SWEET'S
SWEETS

Connie Shelton

**Books
by Connie Shelton**

THE CHARLIE PARKER SERIES

Deadly Gamble
Vacations Can Be Murder
Partnerships Can Be Murder
Small Towns Can Be Murder
Memories Can Be Murder
Honeymoons Can Be Murder
Reunions Can Be Murder
Competition Can Be Murder
Balloons Can Be Murder
Obsessions Can Be Murder
Gossip Can Be Murder

Holidays Can Be Murder - a Christmas novella

THE SAMANTHA SWEET SERIES

Sweet Masterpiece
Sweet's Sweets

SWEET'S

SWEETS

The Second Samantha Sweet Mystery

Connie Shelton

Secret Staircase Books

Sweet's Sweets
Published by Secret Staircase Books, an imprint of
Columbine Publishing Group
PO Box 416, Angel Fire, NM 87710

Printed and bound in the United States of America
ISBN 1456533509
ISBN-13 978-1456533502

This book is a work of fiction. Names, characters, places and
incidents are either the product of the author's imagination or are
used fictitiously. Any resemblance to actual events or locales or
persons, living or dead, is entirely coincidental. Although the author
and publisher have made every effort to ensure the accuracy and
completeness of information contained in this book we assume
no responsibility for errors, inaccuracies, omissions, or any
inconsistency herein. Any slights of people, places or organizations
are unintentional.

Book layout and design by Secret Staircase Books
Cover illustration © Geraktv

First trade paperback edition: January, 2011

For Dan.
It's amazing how twenty years have flown by!
Thanks for being my wonderful partner.

Author's Note

Readers who might be familiar with the Taos County Sheriff's Department will undoubtedly notice that the department described in my series is quite a bit smaller than the actual. For story purposes, I've given them fewer deputies and other personnel. I've also moved the location of the offices. No need to write and inform me of my 'mistakes.' It's been done on purpose. I hope you'll simply enjoy the story for what it is, including the 'magic' parts!

Once again I extend my thanks to Susan Slater, for your editorial suggestions and for all the good catches you make in editing my work. And to my readers, my thanks for your loyalty and for recommending my books to others; you make it all worthwhile. You are the best!

Prologue

The woman tensed. Were those footsteps behind her on the dark street? She couldn't be sure. She spun to check—saw nothing.

Catching a whiff of cologne—or was it someone's garden?—she picked up her pace. Where were the crowds? The people who normally jammed the plaza and surrounding streets on these early-autumn evenings were gone. Was it really that late?

She must have lingered in her lover's bed far too many hours. She raised the collar of her light jacket, sniffed it. Did she smell of him? Despite a shower, she feared that she might carry his scent home.

There was always danger in these matters, the constant fear of being caught, the continual deception, even with her closest friends. The stress of keeping up appearances . . . it was all becoming too much.

But he loved her—didn't he? She loved him, she felt

certain of that. Nearly certain. And yet she couldn't break the news to her husband. Wouldn't rip the bandage off and get it over with cleanly. Couldn't seem to leave the miserable, sham marriage behind and start a new life. The time wasn't right, not yet

A scuff on the sidewalk behind her. She froze. Dared a glance. A shadow moved but she couldn't be certain—a man, or merely a tree branch? For a moment she nearly let her guard down, almost didn't care what happened to her.

But self-preservation prevailed.

She ran blindly up a side street, then spotted an alleyway just ahead. On a nano-second's impulse she ducked into it. The stupid high heels were killing her feet; she'd never be able to outrun the stalker. What did she have for a weapon?

She fumbled her purse open, felt blindly for anything she might use to defend herself.

The footfalls resumed. Closer.

She held her breath.

Someone was there, mere feet from the alley. Her fingers touched her wallet, a lipstick, her car keys. They closed around a small knife she'd forgotten about, a pen knife her husband had left in the car. She'd intended to take it in the house. A four inch blade—silly, really, for self defense—but it might dissuade an attacker.

The footsteps, again. He seemed to pause and consider the alley. Ahead, as she remembered, the road curved to the north. For all he knew, she might have kept running, beyond his sight. She took his hesitation as uncertainty. She thumbed the blade of the knife open, pressing her back against the block wall.

What if it turned out to be her husband? Possibly the perfect opportunity to rid herself of him forever, to be with the man she really wanted. The thought flitted through her head in an instant, shocking her. But would she have the nerve?

A silhouette filled the alley. Oh god, she thought.

He stepped toward her. She edged away, two steps, bumped into something. He came forward. Instinct kicked in and her right hand slashed toward his face. The knife blade connected—she couldn't tell where. But at once there was blood. A lot of it.

The man grabbed at his neck and crumpled to the ground. She leaped past his flailing legs. As he rolled to his back she caught a glimpse of his face. A stranger.

Chapter 1

October light filtered through a layer of grime on wide storefront windows, playing up the air of abandonment. Samantha Sweet viewed the challenge ahead of her as she scrawled her signature on the lease. Cleaning up a mess was nothing new to her. She relished the task ahead—refinishing the old wood-framed display cases, throwing out piles of old junk, making those front windows sparkle so that her scrumptious pastries could beckon the world to her door.

Sweet's Sweets. Her own bake shop. Her dream.

She watched as Victor Tafoya, her new landlord, countersigned the papers. The seventy-five year old man reminded her of the Grinch, minus the green. Skinny, wizened, with a shock of sparse white hair which he usually covered with a battered straw hat, no matter the season—Tafoya was known around town for being miserly and grumpy but generally fair. However, Sam would rather deal with him than his son Carlos, who fancied himself something of a monarch here in Taos. Two terms as mayor, now running for governor of New Mexico, Carlos was reputed to share his father's stingy ways, without the fairness. Sam dreaded the day he would take over the elder Tafoya's rental properties.

She sighed and took the signed pages and key Victor Tafoya handed her. The old man grumbled something about how her check better clear the bank or he'd be back, then he walked out without another word.

Sam let a smile spread over her features as she turned and surveyed her little domain. As long as she paid her rent on time and was able to perform repairs herself, she shouldn't need to deal with either of the Tafoyas for a long time. She loved her vision for this spot—and the location was perfect.

"Knocking, knocking . . ."

Ivan Petrenko, owner of Mysterious Happenings the bookshop next door, peered around the edge of the door. A longtime customer for her pastries, Ivan was an endearing little man whose curious mixture of Russian and French usually kept Sam guessing. Rumor had it that he had defected from Russia to Paris with his wife's ballet troupe, but there had been no evidence of a wife here in Taos. She must have found Paris more alluring, at whatever point in time Ivan decided to move on to America.

"We are the neighbors now, eh?" He stepped into the room and surveyed the mess the former tenant had left behind.

"It's going to need some cleanup, isn't it?" Sam said.

"*Oui*, but Miss Samantha is how do you say, up to the task?"

Sam laughed. "Yes, indeed. I am. I hope to have the shop open in a week or so."

Another tap at the door interrupted.

"Samantha . . . it's official, then?" The newcomer was her other neighbor, Erika Davis-Jones—Riki D-J to everyone—who owned a dog-grooming shop to the south. They'd met through the book group at Mysterious Happenings, and Sam immediately took a liking to the petite British-born young woman who wasn't a whole lot older than her own daughter.

Sam held up the pages of the lease. "Yep. Here I am."

Riki squealed and danced around. "I'm so happy for you, Sam."

Sam showed them around, pointing out the changes she planned to make. Her daughter, Kelly, had designed a logo for the shop in Sam's favorite shades of purple, and Sam would use those same colors, along with gold trim, in the scheme throughout the store. A wall already divided the space roughly in half, and Sam had a bake oven, walk-in refrigerator, and all the best in equipment on order from a bakery supply house. She'd not revealed to most people where the money came from for her new venture, but there was sufficient cash to do it right and that's just what she intended to do.

At the moment, though, the main requirement would be elbow grease. The previous tenant had not left on good terms with the Tafoyas—being four months behind on rent before they evicted him—so he'd taught them a lesson by leaving masses of cardboard boxes, unsold product, piles of paperwork and old brochures—generally anything he didn't want to make the effort to move. And of course the Tafoyas didn't care. The location, one block off the Taos Plaza, was so prime that they knew it would rent, in any condition. Enter Samantha Sweet and her dream of opening her own pastry shop.

"Is a good place," Ivan said when they'd completed the quick tour.

"Hmm, it needs a spot of work," Riki said.

Sam laughed out loud. "More than a 'spot' I'd say. But it's doable. I'll call up my old resources." A dumpster and perhaps a couple of muscular teenage boys would come in handy.

"Ah yes, what about that?" Riki asked. "You've not quit your other job have you?"

Sam grimaced. Breaking into houses for a living was not how she wanted to spend the rest of her days, but she was under contract for another two years. It had seemed her only choice when money was so tight last year; she'd really needed the income just to scrape by.

"No, I'll have to juggle both for awhile. Right now I've just got two properties in my care and they are pretty simple ones. I've suggested to my supervisor that he might shift some to other contractors, if there's someone who can take them. But I don't know how it's going to work out. There are only two of us in the county right now."

"Well, my shop is only closed on Sundays but if I can lend a hand . . ." The dog groomer patted Sam's arm. "Better get back to it now." She practically skipped toward the front door. "Later, Sam!"

"Ah, I am seeing cars at my place too," said Ivan, heading that direction. "Pleasing to be your neighbor."

Sam chuckled as he left. It was nice to be here among friends. She had a good feeling about the shop.

"Okay, let's get busy," she muttered to herself, walking out to her van parked in the alley behind the row of businesses.

She shed the jacket that had been necessary early this morning and rummaged among her tools in the back of her van for a box cutter. Flattening and stacking empty boxes, she piled them into the van for a trip to the recycling center. The former tenant's old brochures and other miscellaneous paper could probably also be recycled. Most of the other stuff would simply have to go into the trash. She was no more than an hour into the job when her phone rang.

Delbert Crow, her USDA contracting officer. A new job, and of course he wanted this one tended to quickly. Sam took down the address, her mind zipping through the steps in hopes of handling it, along with her own new cleanup project, as efficiently as possible.

She finished talking with Crow and decided she might as well go out and do the break-in and assess the situation at the new place.

She pulled out the roll of white butcher paper on which she and Kelly had written in huge letters: COMING SOON—SWEET'S SWEETS—A BAKERY OF MAGICAL DELIGHTS. Carrying it to the front of the shop she carefully unrolled it and taped the banner across the front windows. Not only would it conceal the current grime and her subsequent cleanup-in-progress, she also hoped it would whet the appetites of passersby and give the business a boost when it opened. She walked outside and stood on the sidewalk. It looked good. She smiled.

Washing her hands in cold water—she must remember

to get the gas and electric turned back on today—she rummaged for a paper towel and then made herself a list of cleaning supplies to bring from home. She locked the front door, felt her way through the dim space and went out the back to her van.

The property her USDA supervisor had added to her workload was located beyond the far south end of town, she discovered as she looked up the address on a road picturesquely named Hickory Lane. She drove through mid-day traffic, past the little community of Ranchos de Taos with its famous historic church, and turned off the highway into an area filled with tiny houses interspersed with single-wide trailers. The lots were small and most had no landscaping to speak of—dirt yards with a few shrubs and a lot of kids' plastic toys seemed to be the norm. Hickory was the first dirt road after the turnoff.

She figured out the address by process of elimination. Looking for #23 she spotted a 21 on one side and a 25 on the other. The unmarked one in the middle must be it. She pulled through an opening in the coyote stake fence, onto a dirt track that passed for a driveway. The little house was covered in badly done white stucco, with aluminum frame windows and a cheap hollow-core wooden front door. Surprising that the USDA had guaranteed a loan for the place; not surprising that the owner abandoned it. Sad, really, that even such an unassuming house would be beyond the means of the buyer. Perhaps someone who had lost a job in the recession. Sam had no way of knowing. Her job was simply to get inside, make sure the place was cleared of personal possessions and made ready for sale or auction.

As was her custom, she first walked the perimeter,

looking for broken windows or other damage, assessing what yard work might need to be done, finding the easiest way in. That part of it turned out to be quite simple. When she tried the front doorknob it was unlocked.

The door swung open about twelve inches before it bumped against something and came to an abrupt stop.

Sam bit back a few choice words as she shoved against it and inched into the opening. Why hadn't she worked a little harder to lose some of those extra pounds? She kicked at whatever was blocking the door and pressed harder to squeeze herself through.

Ohmygod, she thought, staring into the house.

Stacks of newspapers, magazines and boxes lined a narrow entryway forming a tunnel-like walkway. Sam pulled a small flashlight from the pocket of her jeans and aimed it toward the ceiling. The piles of paper to her left looked really precarious. She edged away. Yikes, if this mess starts to fall, there's nowhere to go, she thought. Even with the unlocked front door, she began to see why thieves had not messed with this place.

Turning sideways, she sidestepped farther into the clutter. A break in the tall paper-stacks revealed a living room. A sofa had some crocheted afghans and a couple of small throw pillows on it, looking like someone had just gotten up from a nap. A cheap fake-wood stand, minus the TV, stood in one corner and little nests of afghans were bunched in front of it. In the corners were piles of plastic toys, the kind that seem to grow and multiply in so many American homes. On the south wall, they were literally stacked to the ceiling in plastic crates.

Paper sacks lined the walls of a dining area—Sam assumed that a table was somewhere under the collection of silk flowers, half-burned candles and cereal boxes. When she shone her light toward the latter, two spiders edged away. She gingerly poked into one of the paper sacks and pulled out three baby t-shirts, size six months. Another sack revealed size twelve months; another size four. Some items were new, in wrappers, while others were splotched with food stains, as if they'd been worn and stashed away dirty. What the heck?

She dropped the small clothing back into the bags and headed for the kitchen. The stench of old garbage filled the small space. Every counter top was covered in dirty dishes, with a conglomeration of pots and pans in the sink as well. The stove would have to be hauled away. No degreaser in the world would cut through that mess. Dreading it, Sam reached for the refrigerator door. Green fuzz coated several lumpy surfaces, but the odor of rotten meat nearly knocked her over. She slammed the door vowing to bring a respirator mask when she came back.

Why this week? With so much to do at the shop, why did she have to get this filthy assignment right now? She cursed her luck and debated calling Delbert Crow back and begging him to take her off the job. She sighed. *Buck up, Sam. You can do it.*

She'd seen a few things nearly this bad, but that was back when she had no choice but to take every job that came her way. She headed back toward the living room and blew out a sharp breath to get the kitchen-stink out of her nostrils.

There must be bedrooms. Could they be any worse? She edged along the magazine-lined hallway and discovered two. A master bedroom held a double bed and crib—both with rumpled bedding and scattered clothing. The smaller bedroom contained bunk beds, plus a single. At least three children had occupied it, with toys for seventeen. What on earth were these people thinking? They could have made their house payments for a hundred years with what they spent on all this . . . this debris. Sam shook her head, wondering at what led someone to live this way.

She'd often wondered what, aside from being unable to make their payments, would lead someone to abandon their home. Six weeks ago she'd encountered two situations where the homeowners had died. But standing here surrounded by junk, floor to ceiling in places, she could see the appeal of simply walking out with a toothbrush and the clothes on your back. Surely the overwhelming clutter could drive a person insane at some point.

She stared into the master bedroom closet. Aside from a few coats, slacks and a solitary dark suit, most of the clothing was for a female. Maybe the man of the house went crazy first and simply bolted, leaving his mate to cope with everything. Sam had been in here less than thirty minutes and she already felt the cloak of despair settling upon her.

Chapter 2

Before she could let it get to her, Sam pulled her cell phone from her pocket, dialed a number from her address book and ordered a roll-off. As much as she believed in recycling she simply couldn't spare the time to go through everything in this house and separate it. Delbert Crow had been insistent that she finish the job quickly. She had to wonder if he'd actually seen the place.

She tapped her toe, debating.

At least someone could use the clothing. She grabbed an armload from the rail in the master closet, carrying the bulky burden carefully through the maze and out to her van. Several more trips and she'd filled the vehicle with clothes, nearly emptying the closets and taking most of the shopping bags from the dining room. It didn't make a dent in the overall clutter but she felt better that the thrift shop would put it all to good use.

The autumn sun was low in the sky by the time she finished and with many of the windows blocked by junk, the rooms were becoming dim. She taped a sign-in sheet to an upper kitchen cupboard, afraid it would be completely lost if she laid it on any of the flat surfaces. She hadn't come across a key to the front door and had no tools with her to drill the lock so she left it as she'd found it, closed but unlocked. She could only hope and pray that someone would come along in the meantime and rob the place of everything in sight. Doubtful she would get that lucky.

Out in her van Sam remembered that she needed to have the utilities turned on at her new shop. It would be too late to speak with the business offices this evening when she got home so she sat in her van and made the necessary calls for gas, water, electricity and telephone.

Two kids roared up on their bicycles, stopping beside her window, eyeing the stranger in the neighborhood. Sam gave them a quick smile while she talked on the phone, and they zipped away again when they discovered no other kids to play with.

It was nearly five o'clock when she pulled up at the back door of her favorite thrift shop, feeling a little guilty at leaving them such a huge donation at the last minute of the day. But Rose, the senior volunteer, took everything with good grace. The two of them unloaded the van, stacking the bags and loose items on a large worktable in the receiving area.

"Sorry to bombard you with all this," Sam said after showing Rose which bags of clothing needed to be laundered.

"Hey, we can use it all," Rose said. "With winter coming

on, there are lots of people who need warm clothes. And most of this looks to be in great condition."

"It really does. I noticed that, too. Some of these baby clothes were never worn."

"I'll go through it all tomorrow." She gave Sam a hug and told her to go home. "You look tired."

Sam caught herself yawning as she sat at the traffic light at Kit Carson Road. Long day. And not nearly finished. She had a torte to bake for a ladies luncheon tomorrow and she really ought to get better organized for both of her cleanup projects.

Kelly's red Mustang sat in the driveway at the back of Sam's property. Her daughter was home earlier than usual. When she'd showed up here in Taos nearly two months ago, jobless and homeless, Sam had given her a month to find work and get her own place. The job came quickly enough. Kelly became caregiver to the elderly mother of Sam's new man, Deputy Sheriff Beau Cardwell. But finding herself another place to live was still up in the air, and Sam wasn't sure how she felt about that. Kelly's company was nice—they'd always gotten along well—and she often pitched in with the kitchen chores. It was just really awkward having Beau over with her grown daughter in the house. A lot of aspects of the new relationship were still working themselves out.

Sam parked beside Kelly's car and groaned as she got out of the van. Rose was right—she was tired.

"Hey, Mom," Kelly greeted. "I defrosted some steaks. I hope that's okay?"

"Sounds yummy. Thanks." She hung her backpack and keys in their usual spot just inside the kitchen door. "You're home early. Everything okay with Iris?"

"She had a doctor appointment this afternoon and Beau wanted to take her. She's getting more frail all the time."

"I hope everything's all right." If it became necessary for Beau to put Iris in a nursing home Kelly would immediately be out of work again. But that was a selfish thought, Sam scolded herself. Iris was spunky and vivacious for a woman in her eighties and Sam knew that it was hard on Beau watching his mother become more helpless all the time.

"Shall I pour us some wine?" Kelly asked.

"Sounds great, but I want a shower first. I'm grubby."

"Oh, right, the new shop! I want to hear all about it."

"What you *could* do that would be a huge help would be to mix up this apple-cinnamon batter and get it into the oven." Sam flipped through her recipe file and handed Kelly a card. "I'll be out of the shower in ten minutes."

In her bedroom, Sam began to peel off her clothes. She raised the lid of her wooden jewelry box to stash away her earrings and watch. When she touched the old box the wood warmed to her touch. She sat on the edge of the bed for a minute, holding it, watching as the lumpy wood surface took on a glowing patina and the small red, blue and green cabochon stones that were mounted in the carved grooves began to shine with light.

She'd told no one but Beau about the box—the fact that a dying woman who was known locally as a witch had given it to her, or the fact that every time Sam handled it she seemed affected in strange ways. Common sense told her not to believe in that stuff. She refused to even consider that Bertha Martinez might have passed along her weird and witchy legacy. But still . . . .. Feeling a surge in her energy level, Sam set the box back on the dresser, donned her robe and went into the bathroom to run the shower as hot as she could stand it.

An hour later, Sam put the finishing touches on her special cinnamon-apple torte while Kelly cleared away the remains of their steak dinner and loaded the dishwasher. Sam carried the torte out to the spare refrigerator on her service porch, where several other deliveries awaited. Chocolate lava cupcakes for the Chocoholics Anonymous group at the bookstore, a pumpkin cheesecake with ginger crust for a customer's business dinner, and four dozen decorated Halloween cookies. Sam checked everything, glad that the little rush in business had happened before she'd been assigned the new hoarder's delight or realized how much cleanup was required at her new shop location.

As long as her revitalized energy held, Sam decided she would type up an email report to Delbert Crow, advising him of the condition of the property on Hickory Lane, letting him know that she'd ordered the extra expense of a roll off, and that she planned to hire some extra help for this one. Technically, she didn't need his permission but it was better to avoid his typical "What the hell is this expense" later, when she submitted her bill.

The email sent, she phoned her best friend Zoë, who owned a B&B near the plaza, with her white-bearded teddy-bear husband, Darryl. Darryl always had a supply of young, muscular types on his crews and she hoped he could spare a few of them for a day or two if construction was slow.

"Sure, Sam. Just let me know when you need them," he said when Zoë put him on the line.

"Wednesday morning? The roll-off folks said they'd deliver the dumpster Tuesday but you never know what time they'll actually show up."

"Perfect. Give me the address. I think I can spare three guys by then."

Sam breathed a sigh of relief as she hung up. She would give the hired muscle a list of what to do at the southside property and then she could concentrate on her shop.

While she was feeling energetic, she gathered cleaning supplies and tools and loaded them into her big Silverado pickup truck. It was the better vehicle to use when hauling big loads, keeping her little van clean for bakery deliveries.

She dialed Beau to ask how Iris was doing.

"Pretty well. Doc says she's about as expected for someone her age. It's just that her bones aren't strong and since she's been in the chair these last few months . . . well, they aren't going to get any stronger. She'll . . . well, she's doing okay."

His optimism sounded forced. She told him about the signing of the lease on the shop this morning and that she would be taking the van in for its custom paint job tomorrow.

"Sounds like you'll have your hands full for weeks. Any chance I'll get to see you?"

"Want to offer me a ride in your cruiser? After I make a few bakery deliveries in the morning I'll have to leave the van at the sign shop and I could sure use a ride back home to get my truck." She had a feeling he wanted more time alone than fifteen minutes driving in traffic. But this week was already becoming impossible. Not a good time for a new romance to take hold.

"I can manage it," he said. With Sheriff Orlando Padilla hot on the campaign trail for re-election in just a couple of weeks, Beau's boss was rarely in the office to check on the deputies these days. Beau was usually the senior man on duty.

"If you get some emergency call, that's fine. If it's a problem I can ask Rupert or Zoë."

"Don't you worry. Call me when you get to the sign shop."

Sam hung up and glanced at the clock. After ten. Kelly must have gone to bed already. She usually left to care for Iris well before sunrise these days. Sam checked the doors and turned out lights. Falling into bed, she wrestled the blankets, wondering if she really was up to the task of juggling all her jobs while she got her business going. She forced her eyes closed.

"The box holds many secrets."

Sam raised up in bed, peering into the darkness. A glowing form stood beside her bed, a wizened face staring at her. "Use the powers of the box to help you, Samantha." The mouth didn't move but the words were clear. She stared at her surroundings. The walls were red, with strange white symbols painted on them. Then her bed was gone. She stood on a cold wood floor, surrounded by small white mounds that formed a pentagram. "Your strength will not fail you and many good things will come to you." The glowing figure vanished.

Sam startled awake. She listened but heard only utter silence in the darkness. Her skin tingled with goose bumps and her hands felt like ice. She pulled a heavy comforter over her and gradually drifted back into an uneasy sleep.

Chapter 3

Bright sunlight flooded the room and Sam came awake in a flash. She glanced around her bedroom. It was only a dream.

The wooden box sat on her dresser, slightly off-kilter from its usual spot. The carved, quilted pattern was its usual dull self. She wondered why she'd even kept the thing after the dying woman insisted she take it. Humoring her was one thing . . . holding on to the crudely carved box was another. Why hadn't she just dropped it off at the thrift shop with all the other junk?

Because maybe Bertha Martinez was right. Maybe the box did hold special powers. When Sam handled it the wood began to glow and actually become attractive. And herself? People had commented that she looked younger, fresher, at times. Times when she'd handled that box. But what about the odd visions? Did she really—

Stop it! Sam ordered herself.

Flinging the covers aside, she got out of bed and stuffed the box into a dresser drawer and closed it, out of sight. *No more of this.*

She brushed her teeth and dressed, then headed for the kitchen where Kelly had left a carafe of coffee for her. Sam poured a mug and downed the searing brew, black. The nighttime cobwebs began to clear.

Silly. It was just a dream. And it was just a stupid box.

She grabbed the key for her van and opened the side door remotely. Planning her delivery route, she loaded the pumpkin cheesecake, the cookies and other finished pastries into the vehicle and headed out, scheduling the chocolate cupcake delivery at the bookstore for last.

Once she had her retail location open, most customers would probably opt to stop by and pick up their orders and Sam could concentrate on baking rather than delivering. Soon, she thought as she left the chocolate dessert with Ivan and headed for the paint shop.

Beau showed up as she was finalizing details, startling the artwork man who clearly was not accustomed to an armed law enforcement officer showing up in his place of business.

"He's just my ride home," Sam assured the guy, although that statement didn't seem to come out right either.

Beau touched the brim of his Stetson and took a glance at the sketches the artist had prepared based on Kelly's initial design.

"Looks good," he said.

"I'm excited about it," Sam told him as they walked out to his cruiser. "They're using that technique which covers the whole vehicle with art. My plain little white van is going to look like a traveling bakery case, and it'll have my purple logo very prominent on the sides and back."

Beau complimented Sam on her business strategy, then he sneaked a little kiss on the back of her neck before opening the passenger door for her.

"Think we might get together tonight?" he asked, with a sultry tone.

She waited for him to walk around to the driver's door and get in. "This week isn't going to be good for me. There's just so much—"

He looked away and concentrated on pulling out into traffic.

Sam chided herself. The sexual part of their relationship had been sporadic over the past month. It was always good between them, but their crazy schedules—his elderly mother, her concentration on the new business—everything seemed to be conspiring against their having much time alone. And now she'd probably hurt his feelings.

"I understand." His voice was tight.

He'd always wanted the relationship to move along faster than she did. And although she'd initially wondered what a movie-star-handsome deputy saw in a graying, slightly chunky baker, the fact that they clicked couldn't be denied. On the other hand, she'd been on her own her whole adult life. It would take a lot of convincing for her to allow a man completely into her life. She picked at a ragged cuticle while he watched the traffic.

"We're nearly at the Plaza," she said. "Want to swing by and see the shop? It isn't much, right now. You'll have to do a lot of visualization."

His jaw was still tight. "Maybe later. I better just drop you off at home."

Uh-oh. Worse than she'd thought.

Two minutes later, he pulled into her long driveway and brought the white-and-brown SUV to a halt. She leaned across the console full of computer and radio equipment and kissed his cheek.

"I'm not writing us off, Beau. It's just that this bakery has been my dream for years. Do you understand what that means to me?"

He turned to face her. "I do." He flashed her the smile that had initially gotten her attention, nearly two months ago. "I really do, Sam. Do you understand how much *you* mean to me?"

Yikes. Please don't let this be the commitment speech, she thought.

She squeezed his hand and smiled back at him. Keep it light. "Let's plan on a dinner out, just the two of us, later in the week."

Sam hopped out of the cruiser, patted the roof of it and headed toward her pickup truck. As Beau backed expertly down her long driveway, she found her mind returning to business. With a quick call she verified that the roll-off was being delivered to Hickory Lane this morning. Next, she dialed Darryl's number.

"We're at the final stage of roofing-in on the current job," he shouted, trying to combat the blasts of nail guns in the background. "Should be done around noon. Want me to send the guys over there for the afternoon?"

"Perfect." She gave directions and told Darryl she would meet the crew to get them started. Truthfully, she thought she could probably just instruct them to clear the place completely, but who knew how a construction crew would interpret that. She might come back to find that the house no longer had windows or doors. "Call me when you're ready to let them go."

Truthfully, her heart was nowhere near Hickory Lane.

Ten minutes later Sam unlocked the back door of her new place. Although she saw the shelves full of old dusty merchandise and the piles of brochures the previous tenant had left behind, her mind's eye adjusted it, showing her how it would look when she was finished.

The wire racks would hold clean stacks of mixing bowls and her collection of specially shaped cake pans. A stainless steel work table would occupy the middle of the room, and Sam sighed contentedly at the vision of working here with ample room to roll out pastry and fondant, to have several cakes on turntables at once, awaiting her decorative touches. She'd ordered a new computer to be dedicated to design work and a printer that could replicate photos or graphics in edible ink on edible paper. She would have so much fun with this!

Energy surged through her as she propped the back door open and began hefting the first armloads of trash into the back of her truck. She'd carried two loads when she felt her cell phone vibrating inside her pocket.

"Sam? This is Rose at the thrift shop? Did I interrupt anything?"

Well, yeah. About two million things. "No, it's fine. What can I do for you?" She wiped the sleeve of her shirt across her sweaty forehead, imagining that her short hair was probably now standing on end.

"Do you remember a dark green trench coat that you brought in yesterday? With all the other clothing?"

One item of hundreds? "Not specifically."

"Um, I'm not sure what to do with this," Rose said.

Sam rolled her hand in the air, as if that would speed the woman along with her question.

"It's got a dark stain, like blood."

"Well, would it just wash out if you used some pre-soak or something?"

"Uh . . . it's more than that. I mean *covered.*"

"It should probably just be thrown away, then."

"Sam, obviously you didn't see this when you gathered up the clothes. This is a *lot.* It's *soaked.*"

She gulped. "Rose, I think you better turn it over to the authorities."

"I just didn't know who to call."

Sam debated for a second. "Here's a direct number for Deputy Beau Cardwell. He'd be the best one to talk to."

"Oh thank you, Sam." Relief was evident in the older woman's voice. "I was just so shocked about this. I didn't know what to do first, and then I got worried about how something like this happened—"

"I understand, Rose. Just call Deputy Cardwell. He'll take care of everything."

Despite her outward calm Sam's thoughts zipped all over the place. What on earth had happened out at that little house?

She couldn't get the image of a blood-soaked trench coat out of her head as she stacked boxes and carried them out back. When Darryl called to say that his men were ready to meet her, Sam decided it was for the best. She needed to give the shop her full attention and it just wasn't happening. She gave directions to the small white house on the south side then locked up her shop and headed there.

This time when she entered the forlorn little house the idea that something violent may have happened to the owner made the shadows seem deeper, the smells more pungent. She tiptoed through the tunnel of papers in the front hall and made her way to the larger of the two bedrooms. About the time she reached the closet where she assumed the stained trench coat had been, she heard a vehicle out front.

Three beefy young guys were climbing out of an old white pickup truck and eyeing the roll-off in the front yard when Sam reached the tiny porch.

"Hi," she called out.

The guy in the lead introduced himself as Troy and the other two as Phillip and Gus. He addressed her as Miss Samantha. She smiled at the old-fashioned courtesy.

"I guess the simplest thing is to start at the front door and work your way back, she said, showing them inside. "Start with all these newspapers and magazines—toss them straight into the roll-off. If you come to any furniture, I'll take a look and see if anything is worth leaving with the house. Any question about an item, save it for me to look at."

The three men each grabbed an armload of stacked papers and headed out the door. Sam watched them for a couple minutes and then headed back into the master bedroom. The closet, which had held all the adult-sized clothing, was still cluttered with shoe boxes, hats, a bowling ball, three tennis racquets and a few wadded t-shirts and tangled belts that she'd not bothered to gather for the thrift shop. She began pulling things from the upper shelf and raking it all out into the center of the room.

In a far corner on the floor, a pair of men's boots were

crushed under the weight of a duffle bag that turned out to contain a collection of paperback romance novels. A pair of sneakers, old and stained, also looked to be the same male size. Otherwise, just about everything was for a female.

As she worked her way through the clutter she kept an eye open for any other bloodstained items, for any sign of blood on the walls or floor. She found absolutely no trace.

Chapter 4

"Miss Samantha?" Troy stuck his head around the doorjamb. "Want to take a look at the hall and tell us what to do next?"

That was quick. Maybe not. Sam glanced at her watch and saw that more than forty-five minutes had passed while she was buried in the closet clutter.

The home's small entryway felt amazingly larger now. With the walls visible, Sam realized that the place might actually clean up pretty well.

She pointed the three workers toward the living room. "This room next, I guess. Strip out everything but the furniture and we'll see how that goes. Then do the same in the dining area."

She stepped into the kitchen, belatedly remembering what a disaster it was. Grabbing a box of extra-strength trash bags she dispensed with the disgusting contents of the fridge as well as the crusted dishes and pans. There were times Sam went to the effort to clean up a place and leave some of the household items for the new owner, but this wasn't one of them. She opened the back door and a window to the fresh October air, and surveyed the room in hopes that she'd gotten most of the smelliest junk out of there.

The light was fading fast, and without power in the house they wouldn't be able to work much longer, which was fine with Sam. Her body ached all over. She flopped onto one of the kitchen chairs, from which she'd just cleared a kid's booster seat and a nasty-looking baby doll.

"It's almost five, Miss Samantha."

She glanced at her watch. "You're right, Troy. What time do you guys normally knock off?"

"Just whenever."

"Good enough for me." She forced herself not to groan as she stood up.

The three guys had made good progress through the living room and partway into the dining area.

"Tomorrow, eight o'clock?" She directed the question at Troy.

What am I thinking. Do I want to be back here at eight? "Just a sec." She pulled a new lockset from the toolbox in her truck, took one of the keys from the package and handed it to Troy. "This will open the front door. Do *not* lose it."

"Yes ma'am." She smiled as she watched them drive away. Troy seemed like a responsible guy, pretty good looking. Maybe she should introduce him to Kelly.

Forget it. I do not need one more thing to think about at this moment.

Ignoring her protesting muscles, she drilled the old lock

and replaced it with the new lockset. Pocketed the remaining key, locked up the rest of the house. In the waning light she walked slowly through the rooms where walls and floors were now free of clutter. The condition of that old coat weighed on her mind, but she could see no sign of blood anywhere in the house. She would have to ask Beau if he'd taken a look at the garment.

As much as Sam yearned to work on her new shop, her body was simply telling her not to. She drove through town, stopping at the market for something ready-made for dinner, realizing that part of her energy slump might be because she'd entirely forgotten to eat lunch.

Her kitchen phone was ringing as she walked in but before she could reach for it, the cell phone in her pocket went off too. Sheesh. The readout on the cell told her it was Beau; the voice coming over her answering machine was a bakery customer. The woman won out. Sam felt around for pen and her order pad as she intercepted the call. A Chamber of Commerce breakfast. They wanted eight dozen pastries—assorted muffins, breads and coffee cakes. And if she could provide fruit platters and juice, that would be even better. Oh, and it all needed to be delivered by eight o'clock the next morning. Sam gritted her teeth but put a smile into her voice as she assured the woman she could handle it. Why did she have the feeling that someone who'd been assigned the job of organizing all this had completely forgotten until the last minute?

Sam immediately phoned Kelly and gave her a list of groceries to pick up on her way home from the Cardwells.

Then she collapsed into a chair at the kitchen table and seriously considered whether to scream or simply cry.

Bertha Martinez's words came back to her: *The box will give you immense power. Use it to your advantage and to help others.*

Sam's eyes narrowed. The dream she'd dismissed last night now seemed to offer hope for accomplishing all she needed to do in the next few hours. She eyed the bottle of ibuprofen sitting on the counter but got out of her chair and walked into the bedroom instead. The bottom dresser drawer where she'd shoved the wooden box this morning stood open a couple of inches. Sam came to a dead stop.

She stared around the room but nothing else was out of place. What the hell was going on? Could the damn box move?

She gingerly reached for the edge of the drawer and pulled it open. On top of a folded sweater lay the box, its dull red, blue and green stones catching the light from the overhead fixture. Sam picked it up and ran her hands over the quilt-shaped surface.

Immediately, the box began to warm to her touch. She wrapped her arms around it and held it close to her body. When she looked down at it, the sour yellow varnish had taken on a golden glow. The colored stones sparkled with life. Her hands warmed and she felt a new energy surge up her arms and through her chest. The aches in her body vanished.

The first time this had happened, more than a month ago, it frightened her. Farm girls from Texas did not buy into the idea of magical powers, *brujas* or the ability to see things that weren't there. Yet here she was, turning to a charmed object to help her accomplish more than humanly possible. She deposited the box on the dresser and kicked the drawer shut. Rubbish!

She tried to put it out of her mind as she rushed back to the kitchen, washed her hands and got out her recipes. Assorted pastries. She would need at least three varieties of each item. And she better go with simple recipes and rely on little embellishments. Autumn flavors. Pumpkin, apple, cinnamon. Pulling ingredients from the pantry she mixed the first batters. As pans of muffins went into the oven, she mixed streusel for one of her favorite coffee cakes and a lemon glaze for another.

When Kelly got home Sam put her daughter to work cutting up fruit and arranging it on platters.

"Is there going to be any dinner tonight?" Kelly asked as she came in from the service porch after placing the fruit platters into the spare refrigerator.

Sam aimed her elbow toward the microwave. "Would you mind warming up that deli casserole I brought home?"

Fresh, homemade goodies for the clients; deli food for themselves. Sam vowed to stop that trend once the bakery opened and her own kitchen was once again reserved for home cooked meals. She set the pans of perfectly baked muffins out to cool and put the coffee cakes into the oven.

Sam's chirping cell phone interrupted. Beau again. She'd forgotten all about returning his previous call. She set her dinner plate down and fished the phone out of her pocket.

"Hey there. Sorry I didn't get right back to you."

"It's okay. I've been pretty tied up today, too. It's about a trench coat that Rose found at the thrift shop."

"Ah, yes. Was it okay that I gave her your direct number?"

"No problem. She was right. It's . . . well . . . a mess. She said you brought it in?"

Sam explained the circumstances and how she'd not found any other traces of blood at the house where she'd gotten the coat.

"I'll need to come out there and take a look. Someone may have cleaned up the visible evidence, but there could be traces. Would tomorrow be good?"

She explained about the pastry delivery first and they made a plan to meet around nine o'clock. It wasn't until she'd hung up that she realized he'd used the word 'evidence.'

Chapter 5

Sam rolled over in bed and grumbled at the beeping alarm clock on her nightstand. Even with Kelly's help, they'd been up until after one o'clock to finalize the pastry order for the Chamber breakfast, and now six o'clock was here way too quickly. She slapped at the button to shut off the annoying thing and flung the covers off. The room was too chilly to tolerate being coverless for long, so she pulled on her robe and headed for the shower.

By the time she'd finished slicing the breads and arranging everything on disposable platters, her delivery deadline was quickly approaching. At some point Kelly drifted through the kitchen, grabbed a mug of coffee and headed out for her job at the Cardwell's. Sam felt a small flash of envy toward her daughter. Most likely Iris would still be in bed when she arrived, giving Kelly the luxury of time for another cup of caffeine. They would eat breakfast together at Beau's sunny dining table which faced out over open pasture land, and it wouldn't matter if the elderly lady wasn't dressed and ready to face the world until well after mid-morning.

Sam loaded all the platters into her van and drove to the conference center where the breakfast was being hosted. Parking, as usual, was non-existent and she found herself in a red zone, hoping that she could get away with it. Luckily, the woman who had placed the last-minute order was waiting there for her and Sam informed the customer that she could use some help. Three volunteers stepped up and soon all the goodies were carried inside. Once Sam had the check in hand she was on her way.

She arrived at Hickory Lane to find Gus, Phillip and Troy already at work and looking far more chipper than she felt. She wandered inside, sipping from her travel mug of coffee and nibbling at the one slice of pumpkin bread she'd saved for herself.

The cleaning effort was going well. The living room was down to the furniture, a threadbare natty brown sofa, two end tables of peeling laminate and a recliner that wouldn't go upright. She started to instruct the guys to toss everything, but decided to wait. Those might be the very things Beau would want to look at.

In the dining area, they'd revealed a table that was probably once a fine piece of furniture—someone might be able to refinish it—but the chairs were a mismatched conglomeration. Sam brushed pumpkin crumbs from her hands and braced herself for the kitchen.

It was exactly as she'd left it—darn it. No kindly gnomes had appeared in the night to finish off the work. The spoiled-food smell had begun to dissipate, at least until she opened the refrigerator door. She slammed it quickly and debated. An older model, not worth much, saturated with that odor. She called a man who'd previously disposed of used appliances for her and asked him to come get it. He knew, far better than she, all the rules and regulations. She'd just hung up when she heard Beau's voice at the front of the house. She met him in the entry and directed Troy and his men to start clearing the kitchen.

"You aren't having them throw away anything that might be evidence, are you?" he asked, first thing.

Sam bristled. "Good morning to you too." She turned to go inside.

"Sorry. But seriously . . ."

"How would I know?" She led him toward the two untouched bedrooms and waved her arms wide to indicate the clutter in the children's room. "This is how the whole house looked. Worse, in the living room and entryway. I literally could not open the front door when I first got here. And I didn't have a clue that there might have been a crime until Rose took a close look at that coat."

"You're right. I didn't mean to— Could we just start this conversation over?" He smiled at her, removed his Stetson and held it across his chest. "Good morning, Samantha Sweet, the light of my life. May I offer you a kiss first thing on this lovely day?"

She raised her eyebrows. "That might be taking it a little too far the other direction. But yes, a kiss would be nice." She glanced toward the living room and, satisfied that the worker-guys were not nearby, went into Beau's arms.

"Umm. Now I think I'm ready to show you the closet where the coat came from."

He followed her into the master bedroom and peered

into the now-empty closet.

"See? No sign of blood," she said.

"I'll bring in the lab kit and spray some Luminol around. Maybe we can dump some of the stuff off the bedding, and maybe clear the carpet too?"

"Let me get the helpers right on that. You just tell them what you want moved, and where." She found the guys and told them to leave the kitchen for the moment and do whatever Beau asked.

Hey, this felt pretty good, having minions to order about. She wished she could get used to it, but the truth was that she did the majority of the labor on most of these properties herself. She took a sip from her coffee but discovered it had gone cold. She'd just come back inside after putting her travel mug in her truck when Beau caught her attention.

"No blood is showing up yet," he said. "But do you want to see what I'm dealing with?" Without waiting for an answer he headed out to his cruiser.

Sam followed and watched as he retrieved a paper bag from the back seat. From that, he pulled a dark green trench coat and held it up by the shoulders. When he spread the lapels she saw what the fuss was about. The lining, which had originally been a tan plaid fabric was now stained a dark rust-brown over almost the entire torso area.

"That *is* a lot of blood," she said, feeling a little queasy.

"Enough that the wearer probably bled out. This isn't a little cut."

"And yet there's no real damage to the coat. No bullet holes, no rips or tears."

"The waterproof fabric probably kept all the blood on

the inside, and the dark color obscured whatever seeped to the outside. It will go to the state lab to see if we can get some answers." He refolded it and placed it carefully back into the paper sack. "Who knows? It could be animal blood. Or maybe someone was hurt and grabbed this to wrap around a wound. That's why I needed to see what additional evidence might be in the house."

"But, geez, Beau. If it's enough blood loss to kill a person . . ."

"Exactly. I don't think they died inside this house. There would have to be spillage outside the coat."

"So . . . where does that leave us with the house? I need to get the place cleared and ready for sale pretty quickly."

"I know. I'd say it's okay to keep removing the small stuff. Leave the furniture for now—beds, sofas and such might be places that a murder could occur. Once we've got a few test results from the lab, I'll know whether I need to come back."

Sam fumed. Getting this place finished up would free her to work on her shop and the delay chafed at her.

He seemed to sense her irritation. "I know. Just a few days. Meanwhile, maybe I can get some information on the homeowners? Names, current place of residence?"

"From my semi-experienced observation," —she looked up and grinned at him—"it looks to me like there was a woman and three or four kids here." She pointed to the crib and three smaller beds, along with the lack of male clothing and personal items, as her reasoning. "As for names, I wasn't given any. Do you want to speak directly with my contracting officer, or shall I give him a call?"

Truthfully, she didn't expect a lot of cooperation from the crusty old bureaucrat and her instincts proved correct. But he did provide a number for someone else, which led to a series of call transfers until she got a person who would talk. That man furnished the name and past employer of Cheryl Adams. Her loan application stated that she'd moved to New Mexico from Nevada. Place of birth was Connecticut, and she'd held jobs in Washington state, Colorado, and Kansas. She had three children at the time she applied for her home loan, but that was four years ago and Sam guessed that the occupant of the crib came along during her stay in Taos. The USDA had no records of Cheryl Adams's current whereabouts, and he somewhat snidely reminded Sam that they would probably be pursuing Adams for past-due payments if they had a clue where she was or a prayer of getting the money. They had no record of a male co-owner and her minor children, he said, were not the concern of his department. Whomever Adams might have chosen to co-habit with didn't show up on their radar.

Sam passed all this along to Beau, for whatever little help it might provide.

Meanwhile, Troy and crew had nearly finished hauling out the smaller junk and the rooms felt much larger and more open with their minimal furnishings. Sam directed the men to remove a few more things then noted their hours so she would know how much to reimburse Darryl for their time, and sent them on their way.

Until Beau gave the all-clear, she couldn't really apply cleansers or vacuum up possible trace evidence or get a whole lot further along toward completing the cleanup. With work at a standstill, she updated her sign-in sheet, posted the required USDA notices out in the yard, secured the doors and windows, and placed the keys in a lockbox on the front doorknob.

The small tasks kept her hands occupied, but she couldn't clear her head of all the questions that ricocheted around in there. Was Cheryl Adams one of those sad cases—single mother, four kids with four different fathers? Was the blood on the coat hers? Maybe the man who'd once lived here, the owner of those battered boots, had been abusive toward Adams and she'd done something to him? Or, heaven forbid, maybe he'd injured one of her children and wrapped the little body in the old coat as he removed it from the house.

No matter how much she puzzled over it, Sam found no answers and the questions only became more and more disturbing.

Suddenly free of her newest break-in job, Sam reveled in the idea that a whole evening loomed ahead—time that she could spend on her shop. She left a voice mail message telling Kelly where she would be, stopped at the first fast-food place with a drive-up and came away with a bag of greasy, meaty goodness that she would call dinner.

The alley behind her new shop was quiet and she parked the Silverado beside her new back door. Ivan Petrenko's vehicle sat behind the bookstore. While it was comforting to know that there were others nearby, she hoped to avoid any interruptions to her evening's work. She reached across the passenger seat for her fast-food sack and the mid-weight jacket she'd shed as the day warmed up. And under the jacket, her secret weapon.

Sam wasn't sure what possessed her to bring the magical wooden box with her today. Before this week she'd avoided taking advantage of its powers. Was it the vivid dream in which the old *bruja*, Bertha Martinez, had appeared and encouraged her to use the box to her advantage? Or was it the fact that the recent workload had left her feeling overwhelmed, in need of any little help she could get? Sam brushed aside her nagging doubts and grabbed it up.

Indoors, she switched on the lights. The retail space echoed with a satisfying emptiness. Sam had made more headway yesterday than she'd thought. The front of the shop contained only the nicest of the display cases, the ones she planned to keep, and the back room needed just a bit more clearing before she would be able to start bringing in her own fixtures. She wiped off a space on an old table and set her dinner and the wooden box there.

Closing her eyes, she placed her hands on the box. As the warm glow began to spread up her arms she breathed contentedly. Alone in her own space, secure with the doors locked against the rest of the world, Sam fixed the vision of her finished pastry shop in her head. What if the box's powers went far beyond anything she could imagine, as the vision of Bertha Martinez had suggested? What if she were to open her eyes and the shop would be there, real and finished, ready to open for customers? What if . . .

The tingle in Sam's arms became intense. Her heart raced as if jolted by electricity. She yanked her hands away from the box.

Her eyes popped open and she stared around the storeroom. Everything was as before. Thank god. What would she have done had her vision actually manifested itself? The very idea scared her. Thrilled her. She couldn't be sure which.

She stood up and shook her hands to relieve the prickling sensation.

Delving into the sack she grabbed two fries and gobbled them. The cheeseburger disappeared in a few bites. She couldn't remember having lunch and there'd been only a slice of pumpkin bread for breakfast. That explained it. No wonder she'd been lightheaded, allowing her imagination to go all vivid on her. Crazy.

She wiped her hands on the napkin from the bag and tossed the wrappers into a trash bag. *Furniture polish—that will make me feel better.*

She went to work on the display cases in the sales room. The wood immediately began to gleam with new luster and the glass shone brilliantly. She'd been half worried that the old furnishings would be too battered and worn to do her any good, but they were turning out beautifully. She pushed them into the positions where she'd envisioned them. Nice.

The old hardwood floors didn't seem nearly as scarred as she'd first thought. Just having the lights on made all the difference, she decided. She swept, mopped and applied a good coat of paste wax. The electric buffer that she'd left here yesterday made quick work of that task and when it was finished Sam stood back, gazing out at her showroom.

Really, with the addition of tables and chairs, a cash register and a few more odds and ends, she could begin making sales right away. She smiled at her handiwork.

Scarcely two hours had passed but Sam didn't want to dwell upon the fact that she was obviously working under the influence of the box's magic. She turned to the second room, the one that would be her kitchen. With the power of invincibility behind her she began shoving everything she didn't plan to keep—every box, every old rickety shelf unit, every tacky bit of detritus that the old tenant had left behind—toward the back door. It made a good-sized stack but she piled it all up. Then she opened the back door and began heaving all the junk into the dumpster in the alley.

One by one, the trashy items became history. Sam didn't give herself the chance to think about how her joints were going to feel in the morning, or the luxury of saying that she ought to quit and tackle it again tomorrow. She simply worked like a robot—reach, lift, turn, throw. And soon the big stack became a small stack and quickly even the small stack was gone. She gave a sigh and took a deep breath of the crisp night air.

Ivan's vehicle was gone now. It must be after eight o'clock.

Sam still felt like she had energy to spare. Secretly glad that no one had stopped by to interrupt, she went back inside and began cleaning the floors in the back room. These were sealed concrete and the cleanup went quickly, as she filled and refilled her mop bucket, washing all traces of the former dust and grime down the drain in the little porcelain sink in one corner. Soon, stainless fixtures would replace the old ones. She assembled bakery racks in her new storage area, readying it for the stores of supplies and tools she now kept crowded into her meager service porch at home.

Stepping back, she surveyed the now-open work space. Last month when Sam first had the idea that this location would become hers, she'd come by with the landlord and measured the entire area. When the reality of having money in the bank finally sank in, she'd ordered custom fixtures from a commercial kitchen outfitter in Albuquerque and Darryl's cabinetry man was making the rest of what she needed—a back counter for the sales area, window display shelves and special racks for cakes and other pastries.

She laughed aloud. What fun this was turning out to be!

Chapter 6

The luxury of sleeping late would no longer be a regular thing, Sam was beginning to realize. She awoke to a gray dawn, knowing that a million tasks awaited, but she rolled over and tugged the comforter up over her shoulders. Dimly, from the rest of the house, came the sounds of Kelly rising and showering and making her way to the kitchen. Sam ignored it all, telling herself that just thirty more minutes of sleep wouldn't hurt anything.

When her bedside phone rang at eight o'clock, she sat up and rubbed at her eyes. Clearing her throat she picked up the receiver.

"Samantha Sweet," she answered, hoping she didn't sound as sleepy as she felt.

"I'm at my wits end," the female voice said. "My niece's birthday party is at four o'clock and I completely forgot that I was the one who volunteered to bring the cake."

Groping for pen and paper, Sam privately wondered why the lady didn't simply grab a generic cake at the grocery store.

". . . princess theme and the cake has to be shaped like a castle."

"A castle?" On less than a day's notice?

"Pink. With lavender flowers and a pony in front of it."

Sam opened her mouth to protest that she didn't just happen to have a pony waiting around to grace this particular cake. But the woman uttered the magic words: "I'll pay extra."

Damn straight, you will.

"Give me just a second here," Sam said, jotting instructions as fast as she could, taking information about how many guests there would be and trying to wrap her head around the logistics of putting this thing together on such short notice. As she calculated the number of layers and the amount of trimming she'd have to do, her call waiting signal came through. She excused herself to the distraught woman and clicked over to the other call.

"Ms. Sweet, it's Maria at Signs R Us. Just wanted to let you know that your van will be ready to pick up anytime after noon today."

Sam jotted a note on her hand. By noon it looked like she would be up to her elbows in pink frosting and cake crumbs.

Back to the lady with the emergency castle order. Sam thought of the most she'd ever charged for a special-shape cake and doubled it, half hoping the woman would call her crazy and hang up. But, no. She accepted without a second's hesitation and gave the address where she wanted this miracle cake delivered.

"Be sure to be there by three-thirty," she said.

"I'll do my best, ma'am." Sam bit back what she really wanted to say, glad she had doubled the price.

All this before I've even been to the bathroom, she thought, grabbing up some jeans and a clean work shirt. Thirty minutes later the first two cake pans were in the oven and she'd gathered ingredients for sponge cupcakes. Stacking them was the easiest way she could think of to create turrets. Rummaging through an upper cabinet in search of pink lace to line the cake board, she'd come across a plastic unicorn that she'd once ordered from her supplier, thinking it was cute.

The oven timer pinged, the layers came out, cupcakes went in. And Sam began piping a host of lavender and pink roses, setting them aside in the fridge to firm up before they could be placed on the cake. She stuck the cakes into the fridge, as well, pushing desperately to cool them a little faster.

Her cell phone vibrated on the kitchen table and then chirped out a couple of final tones. Beau. She picked it up and balanced it against her cheek while she scooped colored icing into a pastry bag.

"Hey there," he said. "How's things going?"

"No time whatsoever for conversation. Sorry, that was rude. I didn't mean . . . "

"No, it's okay. I don't have much time either. Thought you might want to know that the preliminary blood test from that coat shows it to be male. So, it's not your lady homeowner. But it'll take awhile longer to get specific DNA."

Sam felt a degree of relief that Cheryl Adams wasn't the victim of whatever had happened. Still, Sam wondered . . . maybe one of the men in Cheryl's life had pushed her too far.

"I'm working on a few leads that might tell us where Ms. Adams went when she left Taos," Beau was saying. "She has relatives in Colorado, but I haven't been able to make contact yet. And I won't get to it today. Just got a call that Search and Rescue is recovering a body from the bottom of the gorge. Probably some bridge-jumper but I'm going to have to investigate. I was hoping to see you tonight . . ."

"It's all right, really. Things are stacking up on me too. The shop—"

He was already saying goodbye and she let it go at that.

Thinking of her store reminded her that she intended to call the fixture manufacturer in Albuquerque very first thing this morning and had become sidetracked. She set aside the filled pastry bag and looked up their number.

"I've got four orders bigger than yours, lady," the guy told her.

"My stuff was promised for this week, and it's already Thursday."

"Yeah, well, sometimes we just don't get what we wish for. I'll try for Monday."

Sam felt her blood pressure rising and bit back a sharp retort. She hung up abruptly. No sense in pissing the guy off further; he already had enough issues and she certainly wouldn't get her equipment faster by making him mad. She tossed the cell phone back onto the table and blew out a sharp breath.

The kitchen phone rang before she'd had the chance to turn around, and the timer on the cupcakes went off at the same instant. Sam reached for the phone with one hand, saying, "Please hold one moment" as she grabbed an oven mitt and pulled the door open with the other hand.

"Thank you for holding," she said in the most businesslike tone she could muster.

"Mom? Busy day?"

"I can't even describe—" The call-waiting beep came through again. "Can I put you on hold a second, Kelly?"

"I'll let you go. Just wanted to say that I won't be home for dinner. Fill you in later. Bye."

I have to get some help with this, Sam thought as she clicked through to the other call.

"Is this the Sweet's Sweets bakery?"

"Yes, ma'am, it certainly is." *Cool—the new call-forwarding is working and word is getting out!*

"Can you handle a rather large order?"

Oh, god, not today. "What can we do for you?"

"My name is Elena Tafoya and my husband is running for governor. Perhaps you've heard of him, Carlos Tafoya?"

Son of the crotchety landlord, Victor Tafoya. Oh yeah, she'd heard of him.

The woman went on. "We'll be needing a large victory cake. Maybe several. I don't know how to figure out that kind of thing."

Sam sat down with her order pad and took a deep breath. Hand-holding was something she did all the time. "How many guests do you expect at the, uh, victory party?"

Elena Tafoya chuckled lightly. "Oh, you mean, what if Carlos doesn't win? What if it's not a victory after all?"

"I didn't want to say that, but I guess one never knows really."

"Well, that's true. But there will be a party, either way.

Something to thank the volunteers and everyone."

Sam went into an explanation about how many people could be served from a tiered cake, a sheet cake, a half-sheet and so forth. "If you think the amount you order isn't quite enough, I can always bake a second cake that day, as long as it's a simple design."

"Oh, I like that idea. Maybe we could do a main cake that's two or three tiers high. And if we need more, just some regular sheet cakes to feed the extra people?"

Sam assured her that would work easily and proceeded to take the information about colors and style. "Thanks" seemed to be an appropriate message to put on the cake, win or lose. She was beginning to enjoy the conversation with Elena Tafoya when the clock in the living room chimed noon, reminding her that she had to figure out how to retrieve her van from the paint shop and finish the complicated castle cake in the next three hours.

She put on her most cordial voice as she said goodbye and assured the politician's wife that she could meet their requirements. As she was quickly learning from Beau, politics in this county carried a lot of weight, and her fledgling business could use all the connections she could muster.

Sam looked at the mess all over her kitchen—dirty mixing bowls in the sink, pastry bags filled with white, pink and lavender icing, cupcakes cooling in the pans. She tipped them out onto a rack, then made a quick dash through the rest of it to clear some of the clutter—thinking all the while about how she would get to the paint shop.

Zoë. Sam dialed her friend, who would hopefully be finished checking out her guests at the B&B and perhaps able to break away for a few minutes.

"Sure, no problem. I'll buy lunch if you want to do it now," Zoë said.

"Lunch would be wonderful, but there's no way I can manage it today." Sam explained about the sudden push with her bakery business.

Zoë's Subaru pulled into Sam's driveway ten minutes later. "I'll bet you can hardly wait to get your shop open. But won't you be just as busy? And tied down to the hours of a retail shop?"

"Employees," Sam said. "I'm *so* much looking forwarding to getting someone in to help with a lot of the workload. I'd hire somebody now but there is barely room for two bodies in my kitchen. Want a job?"

Zoë laughed as she steered toward the little neighborhood of industrial buildings where Signs R Us was located. "Like I have time for anything more than cooking and washing linens for those five bedrooms full of people. I'm counting the days until the end of this month so I'll get a little breather before the holiday crowds and skiers start to show up."

Zoë loved people, Sam knew, but it had to be hard having strangers in your home all the time. Zoë's upbringing in a hippie commune in the '60s might have prepared her for a large extended-family lifestyle, but Sam noticed that her friend cherished the time alone that she spent in her garden during the summer months. With autumn in its full glory now, she would be bedding down her plants for winter and then giving the large adobe house a thorough cleaning before the next round of tourists began.

They pulled up in front of the sign place and Sam nearly shouted. There sat her formerly plain white van, now covered in cakes, cookies and chocolates. Her logo and shop name, SWEET'S SWEETS, were perfectly framed in ovals on either side and across the back windows. She couldn't have asked for a better traveling billboard to advertise her new business.

"Wow," said Zoë. "I had no idea a vehicle could look so tasty." Not quite the sugar addict that Sam and her customers were, Zoë nevertheless raved over the van's new look. She gave Sam a hug and got back into her Subaru while Sam went inside to pay her bill.

Sam took the long way back through town, making a few extra turns and thrilling to the stares of people who were learning the name of her new shop for the first time. She noticed more than one person in nearby cars jotting notes as she sat beside them in traffic.

The upside of a new business was the excitement of having people discover it. The downside, Sam found, was when they discovered it before you were ready. The phone was ringing when she walked in the door.

Four dozen scones for a tea tomorrow? Sure, no problem. Two cheesecakes for a women's Bunko group? Absolutely. Cider and cookies for the kids at the elementary school's Halloween festival next week? Yikes—this was getting complicated.

Sam had barely enough time to answer the phone and write down the orders, and the castle birthday cake was nowhere near ready. She set the answering machine to handle the calls for the next two hours while she set about assembling the layers and making stacks of cupcakes into turrets. The unicorn finished off the piece better than a pony would have, she told herself as she sprinkled edible glitter over the banks of flowers, giving a magical sparkle to the finished piece.

She loaded the cake into the back of her van, securing

the cake board with blocks she'd created for the purpose, and looked again at the address where she was to deliver it. With two minutes to spare, she pulled up at the house just off Kit Carson Road.

Party guests were already arriving and several of the mothers stopped her to ask about doing fancy cakes for them. Jumping through hoops to produce the rush order was going to prove profitable, Sam realized, in addition to the premium price she'd charged the customer for the tight deadline. She set the castle cake on the party table in the backyard and made sure that she'd left business cards with everyone who asked for one.

When Kelly walked in at eight p.m., Sam had just pulled a batch of cranberry-apple scones from the oven. She was pressing her lower back against the kitchen counter, seeking relief from the hours on her feet.

"I have to get some help with this," she said when Kelly gave her a quizzical look. She held up the stack of order forms. "Seven more messages when I got home from delivering that birthday cake."

Kelly put the tea kettle on and splashed a generous dollop of amaretto liqueur into Sam's. "Be careful what you wish for?"

"Definitely." Sam groaned and sank into one of the chairs at the kitchen table while Kelly brewed the tea.

"How soon can you open the shop, Mom?"

Sam sipped the comforting warmth and thought about it. "It's the kitchen fixtures I'm waiting on and that guy in Albuquerque—ugh—can't promise any earlier than Monday."

"So, let's see how we might organize this," Kelly said, taking a seat across from Sam. She picked up the stack of order forms and began sorting them by due dates. "Looks like some of these aren't needed until later next week anyway. We'll put them at the back of the stack and start with the most urgent."

We? This was Sam's first clue that Kelly cared to become involved.

"Mom, I think if we can get past these next few days, it's all going to level off to a reasonable workload. Plus, once you get the shop open, people will come pick up their orders. You won't have to dash all over town like you're doing now."

"True. Only the specialty cakes will actually need to be delivered and set up. I was thinking about that last night as I cleaned up the shop. The storefront is nearly ready now. But how will I fill it? I can't open up shop with nothing in the cases."

"I have an idea—if you're interested."

"Anything."

"I reconnected with a couple of old friends today. Told you I'd fill you in. Well, remember Jennifer Baca? She's looking for a job right now."

Sam searched her memory, coming up with a skinny little girl that Kelly used to invite for sleepovers. She couldn't think of any outstanding feature about the kid, but then how many middle schoolers really show a lot of impressive traits?

"Does she have any experience?"

"Not in a bakery, but she's worked in retail a lot. Her current job, which she hates because whole days go by without a customer walking in the door, is at one of the galleries just off the plaza. Jen has all the right whatever-you-call-it to deal with a classy clientele."

Sam thought about it. With someone up front, ringing up sales, taking orders, it would free her up to do nothing but bake. And if she could find a second person, someone to mix the recipes and take things in and out of the oven, leaving Sam to simply create and decorate . . . This was getting a lot closer to the ideal that she'd envisioned.

"If Jen and I pitched in, and you were able to keep baking at home until the ovens get there . . . think we might get the doors open by Monday?"

Sam took a deep gulp.

Chapter 7

Little Jennifer Baca was no longer the scrawny twelve-year-old that Sam had remembered. She'd driven over to the gallery where Kelly said Jen worked, hoping to catch her with a little free time for an informal interview and finding the place as devoid of customers as Kelly described. At thirty, Jen stood tall, slender and elegant in a broomstick skirt and silk tunic top that hugged her youthful curves and set off spectacular examples of turquoise and gold jewelry.

Briefed in advance, Jennifer greeted Sam warmly and laughed with her at the memory of the time the girls had tried to bake brownies at midnight and Sam awoke to the shriek of the smoke alarm.

"I'm a lot better at baking now," Jen assured her. "But Kelly says that's not what you need at the moment?"

"Actually, I can use help in just about any way. At first, a person behind the counter who knows the difference between an éclair and a scone will be helpful. Pitching in with the baking, eventually learning the decorating—all of it will be necessary as the business grows."

Sam knew by the way Jen's eyes lit up that she loved the idea.

"I don't know how much I can afford to pay right now. I'm new at this employer thing."

Jennifer named a figure that would cover her basic needs and Sam readily agreed.

"If the phone calls keep coming in as they have been, I feel certain I can raise that amount fairly soon."

Jennifer glanced around the dead-quiet gallery. "Really, I'd probably pay *you* just to get me out of here. I thought I would enjoy working with a wealthy clientele, but they can be a real pain. If they actually show up. The gallery has been just like this all summer, and I'll be surprised if the owners don't shut it down soon."

Sam nodded. How many high-class art stores could a town this size support anyway? She started to respond but her cell phone rang. She glanced at the readout and asked the caller to hold on just a second. "Is there any chance you could start Monday?"

Jennifer nodded agreement and Sam gave a little wave as she left the quiet building.

"Hey, Beau. Sorry about that. I was right in the middle of hiring my first employee."

"I won't keep you. Just thought I'd let you know that the DNA results came back on that blood. No match in any of the databases. I have the lab cross-checking it against a couple of Cheryl Adams's family members that we located in Colorado. They don't know where Cheryl is now but it's possible the blood comes from one of her sons. I should have some results later today or tomorrow."

Despite feeling as if she were standing in a whirlwind, Sam was still curious about whatever had happened at the property on the south side that was now officially under her care. She told Beau to let her know how the lab results turned out.

"Meanwhile, I'm back to working the case of that body SAR pulled from the gorge last night," he said. "When the Medical Investigator's office got to taking a closer look they found a wound. I don't know details yet, but have to keep the possibility open that the guy didn't just jump off the bridge."

They made a tentative plan to have dinner together Saturday night, but both knew that everything was up in the air at this moment. Sam speed-walked back to her van, where she found a business card tucked under the wiper— *'call me re catering a banquet'* was penned on the back in a masculine hand. *Oh god, what have I gotten myself into?*

She sank into the van's comfortable cushions as she dialed the number on the card. She left a voice message telling the man that she would be most happy to provide the pastries but really wasn't set up for full catering services yet. *Yet?* she thought as she ended the call. What the Sam Hill was she thinking? She sighed but resisted calling the man back and revising the message. *Take each thing as it comes, Sam.*

Zoë and Darryl's bed and breakfast was only a couple of blocks away so she headed that direction, hoping to catch them both at home. In her dreams, Zoë would offer a soothing cup of tea and Darryl would say that the cabinetry for her shop was ready. In reality she got half her wish. At least it was the more important half.

"If we can meet him there right now, the guy's ready to deliver," Darryl said. "I can give you about fifteen minutes, myself, then I have to meet the crew at one of my other jobs. Just tell Mack how you want the stuff." He had his cell phone out and was already giving orders.

Sam drove along behind Darryl's big pickup truck, parked her van at the back door of her place and unlocked everything for the workers. Ten minutes later a large panel truck showed up and took four parking spaces out front. Mack began shouting orders. Darryl watched long enough to be sure that the cabinetry was indeed what Sam had ordered and then he headed out to his other job. Sam watched in awe as four burly men hefted the huge pieces and got them through the front door and began setting them in place. The ways in which massive items were built and put into service had always mystified her.

"Oh, Samantha, it's brilliant!"

Sam turned to see her neighbor Riki bustling over from her own shop. The petite Brit wore a plastic apron over bright pink capris and tank top, and she was in the process of wiping suds from her hands with a towel.

"I absolutely love it!" Her wild, dark curls sprung from a stretchy ponytail band and her green eyes sparkled.

Sam couldn't deny the younger woman's enthusiasm. "Thanks. They did a great job, didn't they?"

"And your old pieces really fit with the new stuff, don't they?"

It was the one part of the design that had Sam a little worried, blending old and new. How to do it without striving too hard to match the pieces or risk ending up with a hodge-podge. Somehow, though, it all came together and just worked.

"Well, back to the pooches," Riki said. "I've got a sheepdog in the dryer and an unhappy spaniel who's next up for the bath. Ta!"

She headed back to her shop with a perky step that Sam envied.

"Ms. Sweet?"

Sam turned to find Mack holding out an invoice. She gave a final appraisal of the arrangement of the cabinets and displays, making sure everything was as she wanted it before the muscle men got away. While she was writing the check, Ivan Petrenko wandered over from the bookshop.

"Is nice," he commented as the panel truck pulled away. "I am liking your place, Samantha. I will to be sending customers to your way, I am certain."

They'd talked about perhaps asking Victor Tafoya about the possibility of cutting a doorway to join their businesses, but hadn't done so yet. Sam still felt a little intimidated by the crusty old landlord.

"I'll return the favor," she told Ivan. "But only when the customers don't have sticky sugar on their hands."

"*Spaciba*, this is being the best way, for sure." He spotted a car pulling up in front of his shop and hurried off.

Sam smiled at his quirky thank-you. She stood in her doorway, staring into the shop, fixing the customers' first impressions in her mind. Now she couldn't wait to fill in the gaps and then see their reactions. In the weeks since she'd come into the money to open the shop she'd been buying and stashing away the smaller items. Her home, being an older one, had a small living room which was now crammed with all these extras. Aside from Kelly's nightly addiction to the talk shows she'd recorded during the afternoons, the room wasn't used all that much. Now, however, she could earnestly begin to move the business from her home to the shop. Finally.

Quickly locking up before anyone else might drop by, Sam hurried to her van and drove home. Her answering machine blinked furiously and she played the messages back, making notes, finding only a couple of calls that needed immediate attention.

She still had the order of scones to deliver, and she carefully placed them on the passenger seat of the vehicle. Then she began with the items portable enough to handle on her own—the coffee and tea equipment, trays for the smaller pastries on their display shelves, napkins, tissue paper, bags, boxes . . . it felt like there were a million things.

Soon the van was full enough. She delivered the scones, drove up to a nearby fast food window for some lunch, and headed back to the shop. By mid-afternoon she began questioning her decision not to harness some of the energy she invariably got from the wooden box. At five o'clock she admitted defeat and went home, tired and aching.

"Mom, are you okay?" Kelly asked, the minute she walked in the back door. "You look exhausted."

"I am. But I'm hoping some of these yummy aspirin will help."

"Don't overdo it. How will the shop get going if you've killed yourself in the process?"

"I know." Sam set down her water glass and slumped into a chair at the kitchen table. "Do you mind if we just order a pizza for dinner tonight?"

Kelly placed the call and went out a few minutes later to

pick it up. When she came back with a bottle of decent wine, Sam knew things were looking up. She filled her daughter in on the day's activities.

"So, now that Jen works for you, get her to do some of this stuff."

"I will. I will." *If I can ever get over this attitude that I have to do everything myself.*

Kelly saw the crease in Sam's forehead. "You won't. So I'm calling her for you."

It took all of two minutes and it was arranged that Jennifer would come to the house in the morning and spend the weekend with Sam, baking. They could surely produce enough cookies, muffins, éclairs and cheesecake to make a respectable showing in the bakery cases by Monday morning. Jen would man the register and work out the kinks in the system while Sam supervised installation of the commercial ovens and other equipment. They would consider this first week a soft opening, then plan a gala, a real full-fledged "introduce us to the world" opening the following weekend.

She told all of this to Beau over dinner the following night at a local place known for its hearty soups and generous sandwiches, after they'd stopped at the shop so he could see the progress.

"You're amazing, you know," he said. "I can't believe the amount of work you've accomplished already."

And I can't really tell you how, she thought, knowing that much of the labor had happened under the influence of the box's energy. She'd never mentioned to him that she thought Bertha Martinez was appearing in her dreams. It was just too woo-woo for this solid Southerner to believe.

"Thanks. Will you be able to come to our grand opening next Saturday night?"

"Absolutely. Nothing—" His phone interrupted with an insistent tone. He reached for it and shrugged. "Almost nothing . . . sorry, I have to take this."

The downside of dating a deputy at a time when the department was short-handed and the sheriff was running for re-election, she supposed. She dunked a torn corner of her herb bread into her potato-leek soup and nibbled at it.

Beau's side of the conversation consisted of yeses and no's. At one point he pulled his small notebook from a pocket and began to scribble notes. Sam finished her soup and let the waiter take her bowl.

"Well," he said, finally. "That was an interesting little piece of news."

"Can you tell me?" She'd learned that while he usually didn't mind discussing his cases, relying on her discretion, sometimes it was strictly off limits.

"No harm, I guess." He stuffed the cell phone back in his pocket and spooned up some of his green chile stew. "The crime lab came back with an ID on that body, the one I told you about."

"From the gorge?"

"Yeah." He glanced around at the thinning dinner crowd and lowered his voice. "It was a local private investigator, Bram Fenton. He retired from police work in Arizona. I knew him. Not real well, but we'd consulted a few times over the years. Seemed like a straight arrow. Mostly insurance work, that kind of thing."

"So, what do you think happened to him?"

"Don't know. They're faxing the full autopsy report.

I should have it waiting for me at the office on Monday morning."

Sam continued to tear little bits off the herb bread, eating some and dropping a few to the plate in front of her.

"This might sound really weird, but do you know the first thought that just came into my head?"

He looked straight at her.

"Private investigator. Trench coat." She dropped the bread and dusted the crumbs off her hands. "I know, way too cliché, huh."

"Could be. But it's an interesting possibility."

Chapter 8

Sunday morning Sam woke up with Beau's conversation running through her head. What if the private investigator really was murdered? And what if the trench coat she'd found belonged to him? She rolled over in bed twice, willing the thoughts away, hoping to grab a little more sleep before Jen arrived.

Today would be their only chance to get enough product made up for the store's soft opening and since it appeared that the guy in Albuquerque truly would deliver her ovens and the other kitchen equipment tomorrow, it was important that she accomplish a lot, not get herself distracted by one of Beau's cases. Just because the coat had come from one of her properties didn't mean she had to get involved.

Thinking of the Adams property again reminded her that she'd not submitted her invoice to Delbert Crow. It could easily get lost in the shuffle of everything else in her life right now. She threw off the blankets and dragged her aching bones out of bed. The lumpy wooden box sat benignly again on her dresser. She reached a hand out toward it, then pulled back. What if she were becoming addicted to its power?

Her hand wavered—closer, then away.

Finally, she picked it up. As warmth from the wood began to saturate her tired arms, she hugged it more tightly to her body. Soon the colored stones glowed and she felt the infusion of energy she always got from the strange artifact.

As soon as the bakery was open, she promised herself, she would put the box away forever.

She dressed quickly and went to her computer in the corner of the living room, which was gradually becoming clearer, where she figured up her hours and submitted the bill to her supervisor by email. There. Done.

"Morning, Mom," Kelly said, moving sluggishly from her room to the open bathroom door.

Sam started a pot of coffee and looked around the kitchen. She'd not bothered to put away the large bins of flour, sugar and spices from yesterday's baking spree. The dishwasher was full of clean utensils, ready for another round today. With her newfound energy Sam unloaded the mixing bowls and beaters and began to set up for the first batch of seasonal quick breads and cakes that were usually a hit in the fall.

Through the kitchen window she spotted Jennifer's little Toyota just about the time Kelly emerged from her room, dressed and ready to help.

"If I can get you girls to start with these recipes," Sam said, pulling out three cards and indicating which pans were to be used for each. "I've got Darryl and Zoë coming over in a few minutes with their truck and we'll load both pickups with the tables and chairs I've stored in the garage. Meanwhile, I'm filling the van with everything from the service porch."

Kelly gave her a little salute. "Aye, aye, Captain."

Sam answered with a flick of a dish towel aimed at her daughter's rear end.

The service porch attached to the back of the kitchen contained a lot of stuff, Sam realized, as she began pulling things from the shelves. She didn't remember buying half of these special-shaped cake pans and separators for the large tiers she used for wedding cakes. She found a whole box of disposable pastry bags and a plastic case of decorator tips she'd completely forgotten about. In the new place she would have space to organize all this, rather than simply cramming her tools into every cranny.

"Knock, knock." The voice of Rupert Penrick, the friend who'd helped her recently discover the missing work of a famous artist, came through the screen door. Without that bit of fortunate luck she would not have the money to be opening Sweet's Sweets now.

"Hey, come in," Sam answered. "You're just in time."

"Aren't I always?" Rupert offered a hug. "Ooh—you're certainly tingling with energy! Myself, I'm just happy to take a day off from my writing." Little-known to most locals, Rupert was a prolific writer who remained perennially on the bestseller lists under the pen name Victoria DeVane. He was usually very disciplined in his work, but Sam knew him to also look for frequent excuses to skip out on his writing duties in search of other diversions. He'd been one of her staunchest supporters of the bake shop plan, from the moment she first told him about the idea. Today, the large man had shown up for work in loose knit pants and a shirt with billowy sleeves--his trademark style in his trademark purple.

"The van is nearly full so maybe you could drive it over to the new shop? The rest of us should be along within a half hour or so and we'll all pitch in to unload." She handed him keys to the van and shop and he headed down her long driveway.

Kelly shouted from the kitchen, a small crisis when she couldn't find the baking powder, and then Sam spotted Darryl's pickup truck in the driveway. As helpers began piling from the truck, she was thrilled to see that Troy and Gus had come along. She gave each of them a hug and a thanks for coming to her aid. Within twenty minutes every bit of the extra furniture for the shop was loaded into the two pickup trucks.

Sunday morning traffic was light around the center of town and they arrived at the shop in under ten minutes. Another reason, Sam realized, that this was such a great location for her business. If you had to live half your life at work, at least having it close to home was a huge plus.

Rupert greeted them at the front door, propping it open so the boxes containing unassembled tables and the stacks of café chairs could be brought inside.

"Sam, let me know what you think about the back," he said as the others hustled to unload the two trucks.

She followed his purple-clad back into the dimmer interior of the workroom.

"Rupe, I can't believe it! You've organized everything!"

"Is it okay? I didn't mean to presume . . . But I just felt so energetic this morning."

Energetic? She gave him a long look, but his attention was elsewhere.

"These shelves seemed just the right spot for your pastry bags, tips, colors, and little items like cookie cutters—"

She stared around at the storage room that was now organized exactly as she would have done it herself.

"And over here . . ." Rupert showed racks containing all her cake pans, muffin tins, spring form pans.

"How did you—?"

He shrugged.

"The van is empty?"

Another shrug.

"I'm impressed." He was going to start questioning this—real soon—if Sam didn't cover. Although her mind was spinning at the possibility that somehow her own energy from the box had rubbed off on her friend, she hustled him into the front of the shop to see how the others were doing.

Darryl and Troy already had three tables assembled and were well on their way with the fourth. Gus carried a large box in and set it near the counter with a thump. Zoë had wiped all the chairs clean and was placing them along the wall opposite the display cases, just the way Sam had envisioned them. This was getting too spooky.

"Guys, this is so awesome!" Sam said. "I definitely owe you all lunch."

She glanced at her watch while Darryl and Troy set the final table on its legs. It was only ten-thirty.

No one seemed to notice the time.

"Hello all," came a female voice from behind Sam. Riki Davis-Jones appeared, carrying an insulated carafe and a paper sack. "I called your house and Kelly told me you were here. I wasn't sure whether it was time for breakfast or lunch so I brought egg sandwiches and coffee." She held up the bag.

Sam introduced Riki all around and as the others dug into the sack, she remembered that she hadn't eaten any breakfast, herself. Looking around the shop, which only needed product in the display cases to be ready for business, she marveled at their accomplishment. The box? She tamped down the thought.

"May we christen your new tables?" Zoë asked with an impish grin.

The men had already taken seats and were in the process of unwrapping their sandwiches. Sam smiled at them and extended her arms wide. "Absolutely. Sit. Eat."

Sam nearly had her own sandwich unwrapped when she felt her cell phone buzz inside her pocket. She carried the sandwich to the back room.

"Hey there," Beau said. "Just thought I'd check to see how it's going."

"Amazingly," she said, giving a quick overview. "I woke up thinking about that private investigator, though. Did you get a chance to read the report yet?"

"Too busy this morning with Mama," he said. "It'll keep for awhile. If my boss weren't so busy hitting the campaign trail, taking the local important people out for breakfast and such, I might get more than one day off this week. But since I only have the one day, I decided to spend it with her, maybe take her out for a drive this afternoon. We might still catch some of the fall leaves. I wanted to ask you to come along, but this has to be a crazy day for you."

"Well, actually, things are just about done here."

"How'd you manage that?"

How, indeed? She didn't want to get into her suspicions about the powers of the box. "We got an early start and everyone just pitched in."

"So you might be able to break away for an afternoon drive?"

"It sounds wonderful, Beau, but I better not. I left Kelly and Jen baking at home today. They're probably up to their ears in it by now. But thanks for the invite. Enjoy your day with Iris."

She ended the call and walked back to the front of the shop to find the others readying to leave.

"I don't know how to thank you, everyone."

Zoë and Darryl needed to get back to their B&B—more guests arriving in a few hours. They took Troy and Gus with them. Rupert said he would take Sam's van back to her house, trade it for his own car, and get back home where Victoria's characters were in some kind of romantic mess that he needed to straighten out in the current manuscript. Riki offered to stay longer, but Sam couldn't really think of much else that needed to be done. The dog groomer helped clear the remains of their impromptu brunch and then walked back to her car.

Sam locked the front door behind the rest of them and stood in her shop. Tomorrow the paper signs would come off the windows, to be replaced soon by her logo painted in purple and gold. Jen would be behind the counter, the shelves filled with all the new goodies, and Sam would actually ring up her first dollars in sales in her real shop. A lump formed in her throat at the realization that her dream was about to become reality. She quickly swallowed that lump as her phone rang again.

"Mom, help!"

Chapter 9

Sam's heart raced. "Kelly, what's wrong?"

"The oven quit on us. We had two pans of pumpkin bread in there and it's just not baking. The oven is barely warm."

Oh god, a baking disaster.

"I'm on my way."

Sam rechecked the lock on the back door, switched off lights and headed out to her truck. She arrived at home to find Rupert in the kitchen with Kelly and Jen, staring into the oven at pans of flat pumpkin bread with a much too liquidy sheen on top.

"Call Zoë and see if we might get these into her oven. Quick! We might still be able to save them."

While Kelly made the call, Sam fiddled with the buttons on the oven. These electronically controlled things had always spooked her.

"Zoë says yes. I'll take the pans right over." Kelly set both partially cooked loaves onto a tray and headed out the back door.

"Is there anything I can do?" Rupert asked, looking sort of helpless. Art, writing, cooking—he could handle those things. Electronics, forget it.

"No, we'll sort it out," Sam said. "Go on and get back to your book."

He looked relieved as he practically dashed out the back door.

"Jen, looks like you've got the rest of the day off," Sam said. "Get some rest and be ready for tomorrow. I'll bring all the stuff we've already baked and we'll get set up. Meet me there at six, we'll open the doors at seven?"

Jen gave her a high-five and left.

Now what?

Sam stared at the blank readout on the oven where digital numbers normally gave the status of the appliance. Rats. She pulled the range away from the wall and reached behind to unplug and re-plug the cord, hoping that something might reboot and get it started again, but no such luck. A baker without an oven isn't going to be very successful, she thought. She put all she could into praying, wishing, hoping that the guy from Albuquerque showed up as promised and installed her new ovens tomorrow.

Meanwhile, she surveyed the results of the past two days. Dozens of cookies and brownies waited in bakery boxes on the kitchen table. In the fridge, six cheesecakes in four flavors looked delicious with their crumb crusts of chocolate, vanilla and ginger. Sliced and arranged in the cases, she hoped they would entice the midday customers.

For the early crowd (ha—she hoped), breakfast quiches, crumb cake, pumpkin bread and apple streusel should work. She closed the refrigerator door and hoped she'd guessed correctly on the quantities. Either too much or too little could spell disaster.

So far, all her bakery business had been custom order; now she was guessing at what it took to fill the needs of the walk-in trade. With Jen at the counter, she planned to work in the back and produce decorated cakes that could be ready for spur-of-the-moment purchases. Each day might be an adventure until she got this whole thing figured out.

She placed a call to an appliance repair shop and left a voice message to the effect that she needed to set up an appointment. So many other things needed to be addressed but a Sunday afternoon wasn't the time to reach a lot of people. After a quick call to find out how the baking was going at Zoë's and leaving Kelly with instructions for the finished pumpkin breads, Sam decided this might be her best chance to do what she could to finish the cleanup job at the Adams place.

For the first time in days Sam felt like the bakery wasn't the top thing on her mind as she drove through town. Most of the golden leaves had fallen from the cottonwoods that normally shaded Paseo del Pueblo Sur. October would soon be gone and the grayer days of November would begin. Her birthday would be here in less than three weeks. She felt startled at that realization, that she'd not even remembered a date that used to be all-important. She supposed that birthdays and the passing years either became less important or more important to a person after fifty. She squeezed the steering wheel of the Silverado, reminding herself that some of the best times of her life had happened these past few years.

After a frankly boring childhood in small-town Texas, an adventure working in a pipeline camp in Alaska and then arriving in Taos—pregnant and single—more than thirty years ago, Sam's life settled into the routine of raising a daughter and simply staying employed. Being a line cook in a restaurant, taking in sewing at home while Kelly was an infant, working at a family-owned insurance firm where the owner allowed her to bring her preschooler along. That lasted until old man Sanchez died and his wheeler-dealer son sold the agency to a big Albuquerque firm. Sam, then the mother of a teen, couldn't ever seem to blend the stresses of corporate demands with those of teenaged hormones on the rage. She'd hung in there—barely—until Kelly graduated and then began baking and living off her savings until the job with the USDA came along. What the Department of Agriculture had to do with home mortgages, she never quite understood, but the money was good enough to see Sam past her days of complete frugality. Telling people that she broke into houses for a living elicited reactions from shock to laughter. What she didn't tell them was about some of the weird, strange and awful things she learned about people in those houses.

Now she pulled into the driveway behind the coyote fence at the newest of her break-ins, wondering once more what had gone on here. The blood on the saturated trench coat didn't belong to the female owner of the house, and Sam's half-joking idea that the coat was tied to Beau's dead PI had no proof to back it up.

Sam retrieved the key from the lockbox on the front

door and opened it. Ever since the discovery of the bloody garment, a nagging doubt had hovered at the edges of her consciousness. Had she inadvertently thrown out some important clue that would help solve Beau's newest case?

The house had the stale smell of dust and old food, of meals prepared a long time ago, of things that children had left behind, like dirty mouths wiped on a towel and the towel thrown into a corner and forgotten, of diapers and spit-up. Although Sam had spent hours working on the place already, there was still much to be done before it could hope to appeal to a buyer.

She sighed and wondered where to start first. Beau probably wouldn't want her to throw out anything more, now that he was actively looking for the homeowner's whereabouts. Although he knew Cheryl Adams wasn't the victim, he couldn't exactly rule her out as a suspect.

Perhaps she could help. Sam summoned up residual energy from her morning encounter with the wooden box but the initial burst of energy had dissipated. Odd. Just when she thought she'd pegged the results; normally she got about twelve hours of vigor after handling the box. Had she somehow given it away? All her friends had certainly moved at top speed this morning. Maybe Sam had transferred power to them in some way. She wandered into the kitchen, frustrated with the uselessness of dwelling on it.

Jerking open the first of the kitchen drawers she rummaged through mismatched flatware and utensils. The next contained two rolls of plastic wrap and a wadded paper napkin and seventeen twist ties. Sam berated herself for actually counting them. The third drawer was the junk drawer.

She scooped the contents onto the countertop and began to poke around. A scrap of paper, business card, old mail . . . she hoped to come up with something that might provide a connection to wherever the Adams's went. Delbert Crow had told her that Cheryl Adams skipped around a lot. But the drawer yielded nothing.

Undeterred, Sam closed that one and started on another promising drawer, crammed full. Her mother used to comment on her tenacity—picking at a thread, she called it. As in, "Samantha, set that problem aside—you're always pickin' at a thread."

But this drawer, too, contained only kitchen stuff, the detritus of old bottle caps and plastic devices that only the inventor of such could name—was it an egg separator or a measuring spoon? No one seemed to ever go through these little rat-stashes and throw out any of it.

Giving up on the kitchen, Sam went into the master bedroom where a dresser showed promise. The top two drawers were empty—at least the lady had taken her necessaries along with her. The next drawer contained a collection of t-shirts and pullover tops, most of which were worn so threadbare it was easy to see why they'd not made Cheryl's cut in the choosing up of which clothes to take with her. Sam rummaged through them but found nothing other than the battered clothing.

She hit the jackpot with the bottom drawer, apparently the place of Cheryl's filing system, such as it was. A couple of envelopes with Final Notice stamped in red lay on top of the hodgepodge. Both were still sealed, one from the electric co-op and the other from the mortgage company. Beneath those were other notices from the same, each with increasingly dire warnings about how they better get some money, and soon. Obviously, Cheryl Adams had gotten her fill of being chewed out in writing and simply chose to ignore everything after a certain point. Sam stacked the pages neatly and set them aside.

Below the nasty past-due notices were a collection of pay stubs, which Sam gathered, noting that the most recent was dated back in June. If Adams had been out of work that long, it certainly explained why she couldn't pay her bills and why she felt compelled to walk out on her mortgage.

The rest of the drawer's contents consisted of important things like a two-year-old *TV Guide* and four restaurant takeout menus from Seattle along with random bits of memorabilia—a small diary like an adolescent might keep, birthday cards, news clippings, a Christmas ornament, a snowflake cut from paper and sprinkled with glitter and a blue baby bootie. Surprised that Adams hadn't taken those things, Sam pushed the little items to one corner and picked up the diary.

As she might have guessed, the early pages of the book were filled with the looping handwriting of a teen and the entries consisted of things like "School was a drag today" and "Had a huge fight with Sandy. I hate her!!!" After twenty pages or so, the rest were blank. As Sam started to drop the book back into the drawer a small bit of newspaper slipped out of the back of it. She picked it up.

A marriage notice: Cheryl Tercel wed to Dan Adams. No photo or real write-up, just the simple announcement that probably came from the county records of some unnamed place.

Sam picked up the other two clippings that had been among the assortment of papers. One was an article about Hudson County Rodeo and the naming of that year's queen and princesses. One of the princesses in the court was a Sally Tercel. There was no Hudson County in New Mexico, so this came from somewhere else. The other clipping also contained the name Tercel in a story about a man killed in a car accident, just outside a town called Andersonville. Sam had no idea where any of these places were but maybe Beau could use the information to track down the Tercel family and somehow find out Cheryl's current location. She added the newspaper bits to the stack with the past due bills and closed the drawer on the rest of the clutter.

Another thirty minutes poking about the many cubbyholes in the house but nowhere did Sam come across the name Bram Fenton nor any mention of a private investigator, outside of one Sue Grafton novel, coated in dust, under a living room end table.

Gathering the small stack of envelopes and clippings she'd found in the bedroom, Sam locked the place up again and headed out to her truck. She speed-dialed Beau's cell phone and filled him in on the findings at the house.

"I can bring you the papers I collected, if you like."

"Any chance I could take you to dinner tonight?"

The hope in his voice tore at her. She'd certainly been the neglectful one in the relationship in recent weeks. But exhaustion was quickly overtaking her.

"I've got an early morning tomorrow. First day for Sweet's Sweets and all that."

"How about I meet you at Michael's Kitchen in fifteen minutes? Mama's had her dinner already and she'll be perfectly happy in front of the TV for an hour or so. You bring the papers and we'll call it an early dinner."

An image of the stuffed sopapillas at Michael's came into her head and she could almost smell the green chile.

Practically salivating, she agreed. Maybe it's just what I need, she thought as she started her truck.

When Beau walked into the restaurant, two minutes behind her, she knew she'd made the right decision. He lit up when he saw her. When the model-handsome deputy sheriff first showed an interest in Sam she couldn't understand the attraction on his part. Any woman under eighty would be drawn in by the ocean-blue eyes, the dark hair with touches of gray at the temples and the smile that tilted upward at one side. It had taken some sweet Southern talk for him to convince her that she—chubby, graying, and five years older than he—was attractive to him. Since they'd begun dating early this autumn she'd finally begun to believe his sincerity.

"Hey there," he whispered as he leaned close to give her a kiss beside her left ear. He took a seat across from her and reached over to take her hand. "I've missed you."

"We just had dinner the other night," she reminded.

"It's not the dining room where I'm missing you." His eyebrows wiggled.

A young Hispanic waitress appeared and they placed orders without having to look at the menus.

"Busy week," Sam said as the girl walked away. "But I can't believe how much we've gotten done." She told him how many friends had shown up this morning and how quickly the shop was shaping up.

"How is this being a retail baker going to affect your schedule?"

"Let's just say that early dinners may become a way of life for awhile. I've hired an assistant who will work the sales counter, but most of the baking has to happen early in the mornings. If things go well, I'll hire another baker—soon, I hope—and then I won't have to put in the *really* early hours."

He squeezed her hand again and let go as the waitress brought their glasses of iced tea.

"Oh, before I forget . . ." Sam rummaged in her pack and brought out the banded stack of papers she'd taken from Cheryl Adams's house. "I don't know if these small clues will help."

"Anything's better than nothing," he said. "It could put us that much closer to finding her."

Their plates arrived and a few minutes of silence passed as they cut into the steaming mixture of sopapilla, meat, beans, cheese and chile.

"How did anyone figure out that frying a little square of bread could turn out so delicious?" Sam mumbled through a bite.

Beau's eyes actually rolled upward as he savored the heady blend of flavors.

"I have to stop to breathe," Sam said, setting her fork down after a few minutes.

"I stopped by the office and read Fenton Bram's autopsy report." Beau had paused to take another sip of his tea. "The fatal wound wasn't caused by his fall from the bridge. He had a nasty gash on the side of his neck that hit the carotid artery. He was bleeding heavily before he ever made the leap."

"How could he . . .?"

"Get out to the middle of the bridge and jump off, when he was probably getting weaker by the second?"

She nodded.

"No idea. But the mystery gets deeper. I had them compare DNA in that trench coat with the vic's DNA. It's a match. So, a guy is bleeding out, but his coat manages to get hung up in a closet on the south side of town, while he's standing on the gorge bridge on the northwest side of town."

"He was wearing the coat when he got this fatal cut?"

"Almost certainly. It's a lot of blood. But he didn't have the coat on when he hit the bottom of the gorge. Obviously."

"So there was someone else with him? Who?"

"That, darlin, is the sixty-four thousand dollar question."

Chapter 10

Sam took up her fork again and picked at her food. Suddenly, her appetite seemed to have waned.

"I went through the Adams house pretty thoroughly this afternoon. Didn't find anything with Bram Fenton's name on it, no papers referring to an investigator or a legal case or anything. How would his coat end up at her house if they had no ties whatsoever?"

"We don't know that they didn't," Beau said. His own appetite seemed fine, Sam noticed. He was more than halfway through his meal. "They might have been friends or one-time neighbors . . . people can know each other in the most obscure ways."

She gave that some thought. "Lovers, maybe? Remember, there were other items of male clothing in the house too."

"And love relationships gone bad are always good motive for murder."

"True." Thinking of the many ways in which people who profess to love each other end up doing harm, she wondered if that was just one more reason she'd avoided falling in love, all these years.

Beau glanced at his watch. "Well, my unofficial dinner break has to come to an end. I don't dare take the chance that Mama would try to get out of her wheelchair alone."

"Me too. I've got a kitchen full of baked goods that have to be packed up and ready to arrive at the shop by six in the morning. And I have a feeling that our first day will reveal all the glitches and little forgotten items."

"Anything I can do to help?"

"Come by for a cup of our signature coffee in the morning and have a pastry. It'll look good to have some cars out front."

"Even if it's a sheriff's department cruiser?"

"I think we can handle that." In a town this size it had to be pretty common news that the baker was dating the deputy sheriff. And whoever didn't know about it already would be in on the secret after the bakery had been open a week.

They walked out to the parking lot together and indulged in kisses that became longer and more intense by the minute. Just short of a full make-out session, and saying to hell with their other responsibilities, they came up for air.

"I *really* better be getting home," Sam said.

"Maybe I could call you later? At this point even phone sex probably wouldn't be half bad."

She laughed and ran her hands down his chest. "Nope. I'm going to be sound asleep by the time it's dark."

Beau's Explorer turned left and Sam watched him round

the curve in the road in her rearview mirror. Darnit. He'd stirred up her hormones again.

A five o'clock alarm is an awful thing. Sam sat up in the dark and hit the button, going against every instinct in her body. What on earth was she thinking, getting into a business that required such ungodly hours?

Her feet dragged her toward the bathroom where she took the chilliest shower she could tolerate and then swished her mouth with the strongest mouthwash in the house. If that didn't wake her up she didn't know what would.

She began toting boxes of cookies and cheesecakes out to the van while coffee brewed. The new, fancy coffee machine at the bakery had not even been put through a trial run yet but she needed her vital first caffeine of the day, right now.

With the van loaded and a travel mug filled with French roast, Sam drove the few blocks and parked her traveling billboard right in front of the shop. Until her regular signage was installed this was the best way to attract attention. Within five minutes Jennifer arrived and the two women began carrying everything inside.

"Look in the back room," Sam said as she began arranging pastries onto trays on the wire shelves inside her display cases. "I have some generic Grand Opening banners that we can put in the windows to replace those paper ones that say Coming Soon."

Jen was back in two minutes and began switching the signs. Sam was glad to see her new assistant take the initiative, without further instruction. She started the coffee maker and set up more filters and beans for subsequent batches. Meanwhile, Sam cut a couple of slices of each cheesecake flavor into small sample-sized pieces and arranged them on a plate near the register. At seven, sharp, they were ready to turn on all the lights and open the doors.

Jen had no sooner hit the light switch than a woman appeared at the door. "Are you open for business yet?" she asked.

Sam and Jen exchanged smiles. "Absolutely!"

The lady came in and immediately asked for some of that heavenly coffee that she said she could smell from the street. While she browsed the muffins, Sam noticed that Beau had pulled up out front in his Department SUV. The woman took her coffee and a cranberry muffin to one of the tables, pulling out the morning newspaper and settling in.

Beau gave Sam a discreet thumbs-up when he saw that he wasn't the first customer. He made a lot of noise over the cheesecakes, and another customer who'd just stepped inside immediately ordered a slice of each flavor, to go. While Jen boxed them up, Sam signaled Beau to step into the kitchen.

"So far, so good," he said.

"Exciting! I hope it keeps up like this for awhile. Jen's doing a great job at handling the counter and I need to start on the plans for the gala opening party on Saturday. You'll be here?"

He nodded and reached out to squeeze her hand.

"And bring Iris."

"Absolutely. She's your biggest cookie fan out there."

"Hang around awhile if you'd like," she said. "Get some coffee—"

"I wish I could stay awhile, but duty calls."

"Hey, take a box of those mini-muffins for the office. My treat. Just tell everyone where you got them."

"Deal."

They walked back into the shop and Sam loaded a box with muffins and cookies. Cheapest form of advertising, she thought, remembering that she still needed to give the ad rep at the radio station a call today. By the time Beau left, six more customers had come and gone, according to Jen. A muffin here, a croissant there—it was beginning to add up.

At nine, when Mysterious Happenings opened, Sam had made up a plate of cookie samples and taken them over to Ivan to hand out to his customers throughout the day. And she took another plate to Riki at Puppy Chic. "Just tell everyone where you got them," she repeated to each of them.

By midmorning things settled a little out front and Sam went into the back room to make some follow-up calls. First to the fixture company where the man answering the phone assured her that his crew was on the way to Taos and should be arriving anytime. Fuming a little, Sam had no choice but to hope that was true. Her next call was to the radio station's ad representative. He played the first take of her ad over the phone and she was pleased with the way it sounded. One small change of wording and she okayed it to begin running on Thursday before the Saturday gala.

She was jotting down names for a guest list when she heard a large truck drive up behind the building. At last!

Two hours and a few swear words later, after dealing with all the joys of installing modern appliances in an older building, the delivery men left. Now it was up to Darryl and his crew to plumb the water lines for the sinks and hook up the existing gas lines to the ovens. Technically, a town inspector had to check the work and sign off on everything before she could prepare food here, and Sam was beginning to fret over that since the death of her oven at home, but Darryl came to the rescue.

In true New Mexico tradition, the burly contractor phoned the uncle of a brother-in-law of one of his crew, who just happened to be the inspector they needed. Sam left the room, nearly in despair, when she overheard the part about the guy's schedule being backed up for a minimum of two weeks. She absolutely could not deal with this!

She speed-walked around the block, letting the chill October air blast through her thin shirt, her reward for stomping out without remembering her jacket. The frigid air cleared her head enough to remind her that she better pursue repairs to her home oven.

When she got back to the shop, hands tingling and lips nearly blue, Darryl informed her that the inspector would be there in thirty minutes.

"Don't ask," he said.

She closed her gaping mouth and just let him proceed to direct his guys in the final few steps to complete the installation. A call to the appliance repair shop netted a vague promise that someone could probably get out to her house by the end of the week.

Don't stress over things you can't change, she muttered to herself.

"What?" Jen called from the front of the bakery.

Sam found her assistant wiping the tables with disinfectant spray, taking advantage of a small lull in the traffic.

"Nothing," Sam said, placing an arm around Jen's

shoulders. "Thanks so much. You've been a real godsend to me today."

The younger woman smiled. "I'm loving it here. Staying busy is so much better than what I was doing before."

"Now if I could just find a clone of you, one with baking skills, I'd feel like I could take a deep breath without falling behind in my schedule."

"Seriously? If you want more help right away, I know someone."

"It would probably just be part time at first," Sam said, realizing that she had no idea how many people she could afford to hire.

"I'm sure Becky could use whatever time you can offer."

"Becky? Little Becky Gurule that you and Kelly were in Girl Scouts with?"

Jennifer laughed. "Well, she's Becky Harper now and she has two kids in school. Her little boy just started first grade this year and Becky's feeling kind of lost without the patter of little feet."

Sam tended to forget that these little girls were now in their thirties and it made perfect sense that they could be wives and mothers. She'd had a school-aged child at that time in her own life. By now she could very well be a grandmother, herself. She stifled that thought and asked Jen to write down Becky's phone number for her.

"Let me see when we'll have our kitchen functioning before I make a commitment," she said.

She ducked into the back room again and saw that the men were putting their tools away. The new stainless steel baking ovens fit perfectly into the space where she'd envisioned them. And the big double-capacity sinks would be such a help when large bowls and all the utensils began to pile up. She gave Darryl a huge grin as he dismissed his crew.

"What do I owe you?" she asked, looking around for his invoice.

"Consider it a house-warming present. Or maybe that's a shop-warming present."

"Oh, no, no, no. You can't be giving away your services. You've got expenses," she said, nodding toward the workers.

"It was a slow afternoon. We're waiting on an inspection on that house before we can go to the next phase." He shook his head wryly.

Sam laughed. "Call Gus's brother-in-law again?"

"I wish it was the same guy." He set a toolbox near the back door. "Hey, I'll tell you what I *will* let you do. Maybe a cup of coffee and a cookie or something while we wait for the inspector to show up? No doubt he'll give you some kind of little punch list of things to fix, an excuse to delay you until he can come back again. There shouldn't be much and I'll hang around and fix it as he goes. That way we can hope to get you signed off yet today."

Sam grabbed his arm and led him into the front of the shop. "Your wish is my command. Take anything you want—everything you want! Jen, how fresh is that coffee?"

"I just brewed a new pot. It's that time of afternoon when a lot of people want a little break."

"Perfect. Pour the biggest mug we have for Darryl."

She watched the white-haired bear of a man settle at one of the tables with a slice of pumpkin cheesecake.

"The place is looking great, Sam. Zoë better get over here to see it."

"Send her anytime. But it'll be better later in the week." She told him about the new awning that would go across the front of the shop, the large sign for the front of the building and the smaller, painted signs on the windows. "You guys are coming to the big gala on Saturday night aren't you?"

He mumbled through a mouthful of cheesecake, just as Sam looked up to see a man in dark slacks, white shirt, tie and leather jacket come through the front door. With a clipboard under his arm, this had to be the inspector. She smiled brightly.

"That was worse than a GYN exam," she complained to Kelly on the phone. Six o'clock and Sam felt dead on her feet. Mr. Hernandez was one of those self-important bureaucrats who couched his claws behind a smile. Every comment was, "This little thing doesn't look quite right" or "You can understand why I'll have to red-tag that."

All the while he put on a benevolent smile, as if he were presenting her with a gift. Which, in a way, she had to admit he was. He could have remained adamant about not even showing up for two more weeks.

Thank heaven for Darryl. He'd played the game as well as she could imagine it being done. Jumping when the inspector said jump, fixing each small item as it was pointed out (turning the soap dispenser to face forward instead of to the right, for pete's sake!); knowing when the guy was being plain unreasonable and putting up a polite argument; knowing when the man was flat-out wrong and pointing to the rule book when necessary. Sam could have never done it without the contractor's help. She made a mental note to think of a suitable thank-you gift.

"What can I do to help?" Kelly asked. "I could start something for dinner."

"That would be wonderful—something light. Just look in the freezer and pantry and see what's there. I can't think right now. Just remember the oven's on the fritz."

Kelly assured her that she could find something. Sam hung up and then realized that she'd never gotten around to calling Becky Harper. At the moment she couldn't imagine how she would manage to be open another day without some additional help. Jen had agreed, before leaving, to come in early again in the morning. But Sam just about despaired when she looked at the nearly empty display cases. She took a quick inventory and decided on the recipes she could make most quickly to assure that the store wasn't bare by opening time at seven a.m.

How would she do this every day and manage to throw a big party just five days from now?

Chapter 11

It was time for the box. Sam lay in the bathtub, soaking the ache from her muscles, barely remembering the dinner Kelly had prepared—grilled chicken and fresh veggies. Where had those come from? She couldn't remember shopping for food in at least a week. She closed her eyes, breathing the herbal scent of the bubbles that floated up to her neck.

I simply can not keep up at this pace without some help, she decided. *Take it a day at a time, and you'll get used to it,* her other half said.

Sometime between leaving the shop and arriving here in this bathtub she'd phoned Becky Harper. The timing was bad—Becky no doubt in the middle of making dinner for her family, kids screeching in the background, a job offer that she knew nothing about. Sam should have taken Jen up on her offer to call her friend and present the idea first.

She'd gotten a somewhat hesitant promise that the younger woman could start work on Wednesday but only during the hours her kids were in school.

I'll use the energy from the box in the morning, Sam promised herself. *Just this last time, no more. By mid-week I'll have help. By the weekend the party will be done. By next week we'll settle into a routine and it will all get easier.* She really hoped it was true.

She abandoned the tub once the water began to cool and headed straight for bed. The beside clock told her it was 8:47 but she couldn't keep her eyes open one more minute.

When the alarm went off at four-thirty Sam's eyes flew open. She couldn't remember setting it and wasn't at all sure if it were morning or night. The bakery. If she didn't get at least eight dozen things baked, she would have no product when the customers began to show up at seven. She sat up quickly, not allowing herself to get drowsy again. She might never get up if that happened.

She turned her bedside lamp three clicks, to the brightest setting the bulb could offer. Slamming her eyes shut against the assault, she felt her way across the room to her dresser. The lumps of the carved wooden box felt familiar and comforting in her hands. She gradually opened her eyes, accepting the light in the room and the warmth from the box.

Although the room was chilly with the household thermostats set low for the night, Sam felt quickly warmed by the glow from the box. As usual, energy traveled up her arms, through her body, to her core. When the tingle in her fingers became nearly painful she set the box back on the dresser.

Changing from her nightshirt to the black slacks and white shirt she wore under her baker's jacket, she checked herself in the mirror. Her skin looked fresh and young, her hair fell perfectly into its short layers. She dashed a bit of lipstick across her mouth and found her favorite gold hoop earrings.

On the kitchen table lay a flyer announcing the gala party on Saturday and a note from Kelly: *Bored last night after you went to bed, played around with design and came up with this. Let me know what you think. Oh, Beau called.*

Sam scrawled a big smiley-face at the bottom of Kelly's note and the words: *Love the design! Print out a couple dozen!*

By the time she'd loaded the heavy sacks of flour and sugar into the van, she was more than ready to fire up her new ovens and tackle the world.

The plaza was eerily empty in the glow of old-fashioned street lamps when Sam cruised through. Thick frost coated everything and only a few brown leaves straggled on the trees. She cut across to the next block and again parked the van in front of her shop. Jen had left the sales room clean and neat; everything was ready for the baked goodies to fill the cases and for the coffee maker to infuse the air with that enticing early-morning scent. She sighed contentedly.

An hour later four dozen muffins were ready and on display. Scones were in one oven, croissants in the other. She brought the remaining cheesecake slices out of the walk-in fridge and arranged them in paper cups, ready for individual sale. Once Jen arrived to handle the customers, Sam could continue to produce cookies, pies and a few cakes. She paged through her recipes—crumb cake, apple streusel, more cheesecake (the pumpkin had gone really well yesterday). She quickly wrote up a supply order and placed it online with her wholesaler for delivery by afternoon.

Sam was just pulling the last of the scones from the oven when she heard the bell over the shop door.

"Sam? What have you been doing?" Jen's voice came through. "I thought I'd get here early to help, and look at this . . . the cases are nearly full."

Uh-oh. She hadn't thought about how her unlimited energy would appear to someone who'd not seen her in action before.

"Umm . . . well I couldn't sleep," she said as she placed the warm pastries onto the display trays. "You know, too excited I guess. Tossed and turned . . . So I gave up and came in."

"It's barely six o'clock. That's amazing."

Sam shrugged. "How about getting that coffee going and we'll have ourselves a little breakfast before anyone else comes."

Bless her, Jen didn't question. She put on an apron and started right in. Working by the half light of the back counter she efficiently measured water for the coffee and pressed all the right series of buttons.

Sam stood by the windows, a blueberry scone in hand. "Winter's coming on. The days are getting shorter, aren't they?"

Jen murmured something about snow flurries in the forecast.

A tap at the window startled Sam and she nearly dropped her scone.

"Beau! What are you doing out so early?" She closed the door behind him, shutting out the chilly air.

"Once again, Padilla's spending the day driving the far

reaches of the county to campaign. Left me with two shifts. Is that coffee I smell?"

Jen rushed to get him a mug and Sam told him to pick something to eat if he wanted. He chose a crumb-topped muffin and joined Sam at one of the tables.

Jen quietly disappeared to the back, mumbling something about checking on the oven.

"I got a warrant to search Bram Fenton's office over on Paseo Montaño," he said, taking a careful sip of the steaming coffee. "Now I just have to find the time to carry it out. We're short staffed—again."

"I'm still curious about that," Sam admitted. Even with the million and one things to think about at the shop, she couldn't help but wonder about the connection between Cheryl Adams and the private investigator.

Beau's radio crackled and he set down his muffin to answer. Sam couldn't make out much of the scratchy voice and hadn't a clue about the code numbers but Beau told her it was a bad traffic accident out north of Questa.

"Guess I'll have to wrap this up to go," he said. "I'll try to stop by later, but this mess could take a few hours."

Sam sent him on his way carrying fresh coffee in a foam cup with travel lid. She'd not even closed the door behind him when a woman in a Lexus pulled into the spot nearest the front door. The car jolted to a stop.

"Oh, thank goodness you're open," the lady said breathlessly, stepping onto the curb. "I have a slight emergency."

"Well, uh—" Sam couldn't very well afford to lose her first customer of the day by being picky about shop hours. "Certainly. Come on in. How can we help you?"

The woman pulled her wool coat around her and sidestepped through the partially open door. Slender and blond, wearing a slim skirt and angora sweater with supple leather boots and gold jewelry, she had that willowy grace and way of wearing upscale clothing that said she had money. She smiled at Sam with genuine gratitude.

"I'm afraid I'm in deep you-know-what if I don't show up with pastries for the rally this morning." She breezed over to the display cases and began perusing. After a moment she looked up. "You're Samantha Sweet, aren't you? We've spoken on the phone."

A light came on. "Mrs. Tafoya? I'm sorry, I should have recog—"

"Elena. Please." She held out her hand. "It's good to meet you. I've heard such wonderful things about your pastries. My sister is conference coordinator at Casa de Tranquilidad in Santa Fe."

"Oh, I didn't realize—well it's great to meet you. I've got everything planned for your husband's victory cake next Tuesday. Would you like to see the sketches?"

Elena glanced at her watch. "I don't have time now. I'm so sorry. I'm supposed to be at that rally in five minutes." She looked almost panicky as she said it. "I'll need about fifty items, just mix them up."

Jen walked in with a tray of hot croissants that she'd just taken from the oven.

"Oh, yes, those would be nice," Elena said. "And muffins, and some of the scones, too."

Jen assembled boxes while Sam picked out the nicest of the pastries and began filling them. Elena Tafoya pulled out a credit card, signed the slip and Sam helped her carry her purchases to the Lexus.

"Thank you so much for your business," she said as she slipped the two purple boxes onto the back seat.

"My pleasure. The shop is just delightful. You'll be seeing a lot more of me." She gave Sam a quick hug, got into the car and sped away.

I hope so, thought Sam as she walked back into the warm, fragrant building. A customer like that could provide a real boost to the business. She glanced at the decimated supply of pastries. However . . . now she had to hustle to be ready for the rest of her patrons.

"Rearrange everything so it doesn't look so skimpy," she told Jen. "I'm going to whip up some more muffins and scones real quick."

When the doors officially opened thirty minutes later, four dozen muffins were awaiting, still warm and Sam was just pulling blueberry-almond scones from the oven. She'd also mixed up the secret recipe for her amaretto cheesecake so it would have time to bake and cool for the after-lunch crowd.

The next few hours disappeared, as Sam continued to mix and bake. She whipped up buttercream icing and decorated four trays of Halloween cookies and two dozen cupcakes for the holiday, now less than a week away. They brightened the display cases and quickly disappeared as parents remembered commitments to their kids' classrooms.

At some point the delivery of supplies arrived and Sam worked like a stevedore to unload and stow the new ingredients. It was such a joy to actually have places for everything and to see her new shelves fully stocked—far better than the old days when every corner of her kitchen would be piled with sacks of flour and tubs of butter and shortening.

"You ought to take a break sometime, you know." Jen appeared at the doorway, brushing her hands on her apron. "You were really tired yesterday. Don't want to wear yourself out in the first two days." She smiled to let Sam know she wasn't being preachy.

"I know." Sam peeked into the sales area. All the cases looked full and appealing. She'd put a few finishing touches on the design for candidate Tafoya's victory cake, and had even begun sketching out ideas for her own gala cake. It wouldn't do for a pastry shop to hold a grand opening without a spectacular cake of their own.

"What time is it, anyway?" she asked Jen.

"After four." The younger woman was clearly amazed at how much her boss had produced in a day but the front door chime saved Sam from having to come up with an explanation.

"Yoohoo, it's me again." Elena Tafoya breezed in, much more relaxed now, dressed in a different outfit that managed to be both casual and chic.

Sam grabbed up the drawings of the celebration cake and walked out to greet her.

"You've been busy," Elena remarked, turning in place to admire the shop.

Sam looked down at her apron and noticed smudges of orange frosting. "Sorry." She whipped off the apron and folded it so the marks didn't show.

"No apology, Samantha. The place is absolutely magical! I can only guess how much work this must be."

You probably can't, thought Sam, but she smiled at the compliment. "Do you have time for a cup of coffee and maybe some cheesecake? I was just about to take a break myself."

"Thank you, Sam. That would be lovely." Sam felt a rush of compassion toward the woman who seemed so grateful for the small act of kindness.

While they sat at a table with their desserts, Sam spread out the design ideas for the victory cake. Elena made a couple of suggestions, clearly things that her husband might pick out. Sam wondered—was Elena Tafoya truly happy with money and prestige? Or was she simply rushing through her days, living to please an overly-particular man?

Before she left, Elena bought a half-dozen Halloween cookies, "for my neighbor's kids." Sam detected a note of sadness but Elena made no further comment.

She shook off the feeling when Elena left the shop.

Jennifer locked up and left at five, as Sam was finishing the last of the cleanup in the kitchen. When she totaled her register she was thrilled to see that they'd had a second great day. Maybe this venture would be a success after all.

She hung her baker's jacket on a hook in the storage area and headed for the van, finding herself thinking of Beau. Throughout the day, their discussion of the dead private investigator kept coming back to her.

Since Paseo Montaño was on her way home . . . on an impulse she made a couple of turns and cruised slowly down the street where the investigator's office was. She didn't know the exact address but it was a short road, and when she spotted Beau's cruiser on the right, she pulled in beside it.

"Hey there," she said, tapping on the door and opening it at the same time.

"How did you know I was just thinking about you?" he

asked, looking up with a warm smile.

"Maybe because I was just thinking about you too?" She walked in and allowed herself to enjoy his embrace. "Want some help?"

"You have the energy to dig through dusty old files after putting in a long day at the bakery?"

"Sure." Amazingly, she did. "What needs to be done?"

He gestured around the small room, obviously a one-man operation. There was a desk with a swivel chair behind it and two client chairs in front. A credenza behind the desk held a fax machine. Fenton's framed license hung on the wall above it, along with a dated photo of a suited man presenting some kind of award to a tall, slim police officer.

"Fenton?" she asked, indicating the photo.

Beau nodded. "I think that was the governor of Arizona back in the seventies. Fenton served on the Flagstaff PD."

Two four-drawer locking file cabinets stood to one side, with a coffee maker and the usual setup with creamer and sugar packets nearby. Everything was clean and well organized.

"His files are the same way," Beau said, commenting on the neatness of it all. "I've just started looking through them. The warrant only allows me to gather information pertaining to Cheryl Adams, since that's where his coat was located, or to a direct threat on his life. We can't sit here reading about other people's dirty little secrets, for our own enjoyment."

"Well, dang. That would have been the fun part." She squeezed his hand.

"Take a drawer, any drawer." He handed her a pair of latex gloves.

"I assume you've already looked under 'Adams' and would have mentioned if you'd found anything with her name on it."

"Right. Didn't find anything."

"Cheryl's maiden name was Tercel. She might have used that if she hired Fenton for something." Sam reached for the file drawer labeled T-Z.

"Check it out while I finish going through the desk." He sat in the swivel chair and continued to pull items out, mostly pens and notepads and other office supplies.

Sam riffled her fingers through the manila folders. Each was labeled with a name, neatly printed by hand in block letters. Although the files varied in thickness, all were crisp and neat, as if he made up a new folder if one should become battered or began to slump down in its prescribed position.

Taos, Tafoya, Tapia, Tewa . . . "I'm not finding a Tercel in here," Sam told him.

But Tafoya grabbed her attention. Carlos Tafoya, the label said. The gubernatorial candidate. What would he have hired Fenton for? Her fingers twitched at the edge of the folder.

"Sam?"

She jerked back.

"You weren't about to pull a folder out of there, were you?"

"Nope." She pushed the drawer closed, just to prove it.

"Anyway, look at this." He was holding up a leather-bound book, about the size of a small ledger. "The whole thing is written in code."

Chapter 12

Sam looked at the ledger's pages. Beau was right. The columns were filled with letters and numbers. But they weren't words and they weren't dollar amounts, at least not in the normal two-decimal-place format.

"What do you suppose they mean?" she asked.

"No idea. I'm no cryptographer." He thumbed through a few more pages. Each one seemed to represent one account, or maybe one transaction—hard to tell. "The State crime lab has one—a cryptographer. But like every other thing they have one of, I'd bet he or she is backed up with work for a year."

"Look at the first column on each page. The numbers are written as decimals but they could easily be dates. See? 7.6, 8.29, 1.31. None of the first digits are higher than twelve and none of the second sets are more than thirty-one."

"Good catch. And it makes sense that he would start each entry with a date."

"Each date is followed by sets of letters that must be a sort of shorthand. Client names, billing codes or something?"

Sam took the book and turned to the last page that contained writing. "If this is the most recent entry, and if those numbers are dates, he last wrote in this book on October 19th."

"Less than a week before his body was found."

"More than a month after Cheryl Adams moved away. So, his coat being in her closet still makes no sense at all."

Sam handed the book back to Beau. "So, what was he entering into this book, in code, right before he died?"

"The answer to that would win you top prize on one of those game shows, wouldn't it?" He sighed and stood up. "I don't know the answers, but I've been on duty since seven this morning, I'm starving and I still have five hours to go before this shift is over."

"Fast food? Let's take both of our cars and meet at Burger King."

He picked up the mysterious journal, stuck it into an evidence bag and carried it with him as they left the PI's office.

"Technically, that journal should be entered into evidence and turned over to the cryptographer at the state crime lab," he said, between bites of hamburger. "But I can see that taking forever and then, even if it did lead us to some important clue, a defense attorney would get it disqualified in a New York minute because it isn't written in English or some such thing."

Sam shrugged. He was probably right.

"You did a good job of figuring out what the dates meant," he said. "Would you want to give the rest of it a try?"

She stared at him.

"Seriously. If there's anything in there that could lead to one of his cases, odds are good that there's a file in that office corresponding to it. Maybe you'll spot something we can use. The guy obviously kept thorough records. On the other hand, the book might just be his accounting system. Records of payments or some such."

Sam pondered that. It could be exactly that. They hadn't come across any financial ledgers, no computer. It wasn't unheard of for a guy to keep a coded ledger or a second set of books, pocketing cash payments here and there.

She stared at the leather book in Beau's hand. The idea of a secret code, mysterious entries, a guy who wanted to pull something over on the IRS . . . But doubts nagged at her when she thought of the straight-arrow Fenton in the photo, receiving the governor's award.

"I'll give it a try but you take it out of the evidence bag," she said. "I'm not being responsible for that."

He held it up. "I never sealed it." The book slipped into his hand and he gave it to her.

The house was dark and cold when she got home. A note from Kelly explained that she was spending the night at the Cardwell's since Beau had to work a double shift. She'd left a stack of the flyers announcing the gala opening of Sweet's Sweets. Sam placed them near the back door so she wouldn't forget them in the morning, then went to her computer and composed an email announcing the Saturday gala to her whole list of friends, as if there were any who hadn't had an earful about Sweet's Sweets, right from the beginning.

Twelve hours was about the limit of the box's power, Sam had discovered, and it was quickly fading now. She glanced at the leather journal but couldn't summon the energy to give it much thought. Five a.m. was going to come way too early. She stuck the book out of sight in her nightstand and prepared for bed.

Elena Tafoya came into Sweet's Sweets again on Wednesday, shortly after noon. Sam had started Becky with muffins—they were simple enough—and found that her new assistant had a flair for coming up with ideas, mixing new combinations of flavors. Sam left her at the stove, making an autumn fruit medley of red pears, kumquats and cranberries as a topping for their plain cheesecake. It smelled heavenly as Sam left the kitchen, answering Jen's summons. She had two visitors.

Sam offered Elena coffee and told her to take a table while she dealt with the other, the crew who chose this moment to install the new awning and signage. Once Sam consulted with the lead guy, she left them to their drilling and joined Elena with a mug of coffee. She wasn't sure why the politician's wife had taken such a liking to her, but she felt that the woman was—something—lonely?

At any rate, when they sampled Becky's warm fruit compote over a shared slice of cheesecake, and when Elena raved over it, Sam knew she'd found a good friendship.

"Are you eager for the election to be done?" Sam asked,

during a lull when the store was empty.

Elena sighed. "I guess it's always going to be this way. I once dreamed we would have children and the family would be more important to him . . ." She bit at her lower lip. "But there were no kids, and this is what Carlos does. He's a politician to the core."

Sam wanted to ask if his political charisma was what attracted Elena to her husband in the first place, but another customer walked in just then. Jen had gone to the back so Sam got up and filled the man's order for a dozen Frangelica chocolate chip cookies. He was dressed in business attire and she guessed that he was going back to the office with an after-lunch treat for the staff.

She slipped one of the Frangelica cookies to Elena, who took a bite and rolled her eyes. "Pure magic, Sam."

"You can be my permanent taste-tester," she joked.

"Absolutely. Call me anytime you've got something this good." Elena's mood had brightened in the past few minutes.

"You'll come to our gala party Saturday, won't you?" Sam asked Elena as the blond gathered her coat and purse to go.

"I'd love to, but Carlos always has such a full schedule. We will at least make an appearance and I'll be sure he knows you are the one making the cake for his own victory party."

"Thanks. I'll take all the help I can get from high places." Sam bagged a couple of decorated butter cookies for her new friend. "Be careful of those ladders as you go out."

The workmen had nearly finished hanging her large sign and Sam had to go outside and take a look. The Sweet's Sweets logo stood out, purple against a white background with touches of gold. With the new purple awning across the front of the shop, the effect would be stunning.

"Bob will be here himself tomorrow," the lead guy told her. "Get the hand lettering done on the windows."

"Perfect." Sam smiled at the way the storefront was coming together. She still needed to make up a few dummy cakes for the front windows. Real cake and buttercream would wilt in a few hours with the sunshine, but foam bases worked well and she would make up decorations in hardier royal icing.

She went back inside, deciding to get started on the displays right away. As she pulled the fake forms from the latest shipment from her supplier, she got the idea for the gala cake. Why hadn't she thought of it before? She would do a large sheet cake base and then recreate the shop itself on top of it. The building would consist of stacked square cakes, coated in fondant with the brick pattern pressed into it. She could sculpt the awning and pipe images of the display cakes and the signs. The street outside would be represented in black fondant and a few evergreens and shrubs would be easy to create with sugar cones and frosting.

Quickly, she sketched out the new idea, roughing in measurements and making sure she had enough fondant and sugar. Made herself a note to cut a board large enough to hold the whole thing, from her stash of wood in the garage.

By three o'clock Sam had finished two wedding cakes. It made a huge difference when you didn't actually have to bake or handle real cake. Jen and Becky helped her carry them to the front and place them in the windows on either side of the door. All three women stood outside to admire the finished picture.

Sam had decorated one in autumn colors—garlands of fall leaves trailed from one tier down to the next, while piles of chrysanthemums in yellow and burnt orange covered the top and lay in small clusters between tiers. The other cake was a confection of white on white—actually ivory on ivory, as it was easier on the eyes. She'd created draperies of same-color fondant so it appeared that wide ribbons of fabric flowed down the sides of the cake. She'd applied a quilted look to the center tier, with tiny pearls dotting the criss-crossed lines. Pearls also draped from the edges of the tiers, and a huge fondant bow topped the upper layer.

"They're gorgeous!" Becky exclaimed. "I wish I'd had you make my wedding cake."

Sam gave her a quick hug. "I would have, if I'd known. I'll bet you were a beautiful bride."

Although Becky had put on a bit of weight since the childhood days Sam remembered, she had the kind of flawless skin and glowing smile that made any woman lovely.

"You'll do my cake, won't you?" Jen asked. "Well, if I ever find the guy I want to marry."

Becky left to pick her kids up from school, and the phone was ringing when Sam and Jen went back inside the shop. Jen answered and then handed it off to Sam.

"Hey there," Beau said.

"Did you get any rest last night?" she asked.

"Finally. Got off at eleven, and I'm back on duty now." He dropped his voice a notch. "Did you get a chance to look at that book?"

"Oh, sorry. Not yet. I was fading fast last night. And the shop has really been busy today. I'll be leaving here soon and I'll get right on it."

"That's fine. Look, don't say anything about it."

"I wouldn't. You know that."

"I mean, within the department. If, say, Padilla was to be in your shop or anything."

Sam couldn't imagine that Beau's boss would question her about evidence in a case, but she agreed.

"I can't say for sure," Beau said, "but I get the feeling that Padilla is wanting to brush this case under the rug."

"Why?"

"Why do I think that, or why would he do it?"

"Both."

"Well, I think it because today he specifically told me to wrap the case up. It was probably a gang thing and will never be solved, according to him. Why he would say that?—anybody's guess. My theory is that the election is coming up very soon and he doesn't want there to be an unsolved murder hanging over him. He wants the electorate to think that Taos County is crime-free."

"And chalking this death up to gang activity would do that? Pardon my skepticism."

"I know, I know. I don't get it either." He paused a moment. "Sorry, another deputy just walked past my car and I thought he was going to stop. Look, between you and me, I'll stick with this until I get the answers. We probably won't have an arrest, and definitely won't have a prosecution, before the election so Padilla can rest easy. He'll be re-elected—it's a given in this county. I don't know why he's concerned. But I plan to do my investigation quietly, and I need for you to do the same."

Sam wondered about the politics of it all as she drove

home. Once again, Kelly was staying over with Iris Cardwell, and Sam had the house to herself. It felt good. Even though she and her daughter got along really well, she liked having time alone. And since Jen and Becky had offered to open the shop, giving Sam a morning to sleep in, well that was just the icing on the cake—so to speak.

She made a sandwich for dinner and brought out the little coded journal. Now that she'd figured out Fenton's method of writing dates, those were easy to figure out. She noticed that each page began with a set of letters, perhaps the initials of a client or the person Fenton was checking out. Columns contained sets of letters and numbers, a shorthand system of sorts.

Assuming that each page represented a different client, it appeared that the records belonged to about two dozen different people. Remembering back to the manila files in Fenton's office, there had been a lot more than that. Maybe the folders contained cases dating back for years, while the ledger contained only the business he'd done this year. It was a theory but again she had no way to prove it without comparing the files. And Beau's warrant didn't allow them to take anything that wasn't related directly to the PI's connection to Cheryl Adams. As she scanned through she found nothing in the book with Adams's initials or her address or anything Sam could definitely tie to her. The answers were probably here somewhere but Sam's exhausted brain wasn't grasping them.

She carried the journal to bed with her but drifted off without breaking the code.

• • •

"Listen to your instincts . . ."

Sam felt as if she were swimming up through the darkness.

"The blood will tell the story. The lady is very worried."

Sam recognized the frail voice of Bertha Martinez, the old woman who'd given her the wooden box. She turned toward the voice. "Bertha?" Silence. "Bertha, is the lady Cheryl Adams? Why is she worried? How can we find her?"

"The lady will come to you. Listen to her."

"Where is Cheryl Adams?" Sam asked. "Is she all right?"

The dream ended and Sam woke with a start, her own whispers echoing in the dark room.

"Bertha?" Her voice came out loudly, startling her.

She sat up in bed, fully awake now. What the heck? She rubbed at her eyes, but aside from a faint light at the windows from faraway street lamps, Sam could see nothing. There was certainly no ghost or apparition or phantom spirit of Bertha Martinez.

She struggled to remember the exact words from the dream. Something about a lady and some blood and being worried. Had Bertha given Sam a clue to finding Cheryl Adams? She just couldn't remember.

She looked at her bedside clock. Nearly midnight. If Beau had worked the evening shift he might still be awake. She got out of bed and put the tea kettle on as she dialed his cell number.

"Did I wake you?" she asked.

"No, I've only been home for a half hour or so. Just unwinding with some TV. Kelly's asleep in the guest room and Mama's probably been in bed for hours. What's up?"

"This is going to sound ridiculous," she said, reaching for a mug and teabag. She told him as much as she could remember about the dream, without mentioning that she suspected the ghost of Bertha Martinez was speaking to her. That part of it was still way too hinky.

"Strange that you would dream about the case, especially the mention of a woman who is worried," he said. "We had a little quiet spell at the office this evening and I did some more research on Cheryl Tercel's family in Colorado. Turns out her brother heard from her recently, said she was really worried about her ex finding her. When I told him this was an official investigation, not connected with anyone's ex-husband, he told me she's living in Alamosa now."

"So, are you going to be able to question her about Fenton?"

"Officially, I can't. Padilla would have a fit. If I ever get a day off, I'd like to. Alamosa's not that far—it would make an easy half-day trip, up there and back."

"I could break away tomorrow. If you would want me to go instead."

"I really need to be there. If she killed Fenton, stashed the coat in her closet, then got to thinking about what she'd done and just bolted . . . well, she might be dangerous."

Sam hadn't thought about that, but it made sense. Although why Cheryl Adams didn't just chuck the trench coat in the nearest dumpster, that didn't add up. And if Bertha was right about the lady being worried, well, it could go a lot further than that—Adams might be desperate.

"—first thing in the morning?"

"Sorry, my mind went elsewhere for a minute."

"I don't have to be at work tomorrow until mid-afternoon. If we got an early start, and assuming that Kelly wouldn't mind staying over again with Mama . . ."

"Did you say 'we' could get an early start?"

"Only if you want to. We're kind of going rogue on this anyway."

"I can be ready by five in the morning." She couldn't believe she'd said that, as she put away the tea and turned off the kettle. Her one morning to sleep late and she'd just given it away.

Chapter 13

When the alarm went off at four-thirty, Sam felt even more frustrated with herself for giving up her free morning. What was she thinking? She brushed her teeth with the idea that maybe it was just an excuse to spend time with Beau, but by the time she'd started the coffee maker and found a Thermos to take with them, she'd concluded that it was really more about solving the murder because the key piece of evidence had come from one of her break-in houses. If she'd accidentally thrown away some other important evidence, she could never live with that. She *needed* to learn the truth.

Beau looked a little rough around the edges when he picked her up in his blue Explorer. He was in civilian clothes but she noticed that his badge was pinned to his belt and he carried his service weapon.

"Only if necessary," he explained. "The badge should

work to get us in the door, and I'll make her think we've got a subpoena."

"Jurisdiction?"

"Yeah, that's definitely fuzzy. Technically, I should get Alamosa PD to work with us, but that would probably get back to Sheriff Padilla. Plus, it seems like overkill when we just want answers to a few questions. It's not like we're planning to arrest the lady."

Sam poured them each a cup of coffee once he'd reached the open highway, and got out the bag of day-old apple cinnamon scones she'd brought from her shop last night.

"I think if I ever get used to being up at these atrocious hours, I might actually like it," she said between bites. The inky sky filled with billions of pinpoints had a certain mystical appeal, she had to admit.

The plan, loosely, was to arrive at Cheryl's house around seven, heading her off before she left for the day. The brother who had spoken with Beau didn't know if she had a job yet. Her normal pattern was to live off unemployment from the last one until it was about to run out. With job skills limited to waiting tables or being a motel maid, the good news was that somebody, somewhere was always hiring. The bad news, for Cheryl, was finding daycare for an infant and keeping the others in school when she moved around so much.

As Sam got bits and pieces of the woman's life story, she began to see why attempting to fit into the role of homeowner probably wasn't something Cheryl Adams was cut out for.

The sun glowed slightly above the hills to the east as

they pulled into Alamosa. Beau steered to the side of the road and stopped, pulling out a map.

"It shouldn't be far," he said, tracing the lines with his finger to show Sam the road they were looking for. "A trailer park. Those aren't usually in the choice downtown locations."

He was sure right about that, Sam thought as they drove down a narrow, rutted dirt lane and came upon a cluster of old-style single mobile homes. Signs warned to watch for "Slow Children Playing" and Beau, accordingly, took it easy. Cheryl Adams's rented trailer was in the fourth row, third space on the right. Crispy dry weed stalks bordered the skirt of the metal shell and a dented blue Chevy Malibu was parked out front. An amazing number of plastic tricycles were scattered about the small area they used as a yard.

"Looks like she's already begun collecting stuff again," Sam commented. "There's no way she brought all this from the old place in that car."

Beau rolled his eyes but continued picking his way through the mess, heading toward the front door. Sam followed, noting the sounds of high-pitched kid voices from within. After the third, increasingly hard knock the door opened.

A toddler with wide blue eyes stared out at them.

"Is your mommy here?" Beau asked.

The pajama-clad kid continued to stare.

"Billy, you're letting the cold air in!" The woman looked just like Sam would have imagined—blond hair up in a hasty ponytail at the top of her head, loose shirt hanging off one shoulder, obvious signs of baby spit on one leg of her less-than-clean jeans. Four little ones didn't allow a mom much time for personal grooming.

"Cheryl Adams?" Beau asked.

"Yeah . . ." She scooted the kid out of the way and placed herself solidly between the door and the jamb.

Beau opened his jacket to reveal his badge. "I have a few questions about someone you knew in Taos. Would you rather we came inside so we don't waste your warm air?"

"Here's fine," Adams said, her eyes narrowing.

"Okay. We're looking into the death of a man named Bram Fenton. Some of his personal items were found at your house."

"Who?" She genuinely looked puzzled.

"Bram Fenton. He was a private investigator."

"Never heard of him."

"There were some articles of male clothing at your house, the place you abandoned on the south side of Taos."

Cheryl's features twisted into a mask of thought. "Well, my ex left some of his stuff behind. I probably never threw it out."

Sam nearly burst out laughing. This woman had never thrown *anything* out.

"Was there a dark green trench coat?" Beau asked.

"Trench coat? Oh, the private eye thing. I get it. Uh, no. No way Doug woulda worn nothing like that. Strictly a t-shirt and jeans kind of guy. Wore a suit for our wedding but that's the most dressed-up I ever seen him." She shook a clinging kid off her leg and tightened the closure on the door. "Look, I got kids to get ready for school."

"We believe the coat belonged to the private investigator. Any idea how it got into your closet?"

"Not really. I mean, I buy a lot at garage sales and stuff,

but I never seen a coat like that." She raised her voice to be heard over the increasing clamor inside the trailer.

Beau handed her his card. "Call me if anything comes to mind. Maybe you'll remember someone giving you the coat . . . maybe a visitor left it behind . . ."

"Whatever." She bit onto the card as she used both hands to grab at another kid who tried to make a break for it between her legs. The door closed and the volume of whining voices diminished a little.

"Any bets on whether you'll hear from her?" Sam commented as they walked toward Beau's SUV.

"About a million to one against." He started the engine and backed out into the narrow road. "She genuinely seemed clueless. Well, maybe that wasn't the right word. Clueless about life, maybe. But not connected to our case. I didn't see any signs of deception when we talked to her."

"So we still have our central question: How did Fenton's bloody coat get out to Cheryl's house?"

"There has to be some tie-in. The medical investigator said his artery was cut by a thin-bladed object, probably a small knife. If we could locate that, we might be able to get some kind of trace evidence that would lead us to the killer."

"I didn't come across anything like that when I was cleaning."

"There were a few dull kitchen knives at Cheryl's place, but I sprayed them and found no blood traces."

"Plus, she'd moved away at least a month before Fenton's death, right?" Sam raised her coffee cup but it was stone cold.

"So if Sheriff Padilla's theory is correct and it was a gang killing, what are the odds of finding either the knife or the person it belonged to? Wouldn't it have to be a very distinctive knife to tie it to any certain guy?"

"Pretty much. And what are the odds of us ever finding it? You've seen that gorge. Miles and miles of boulders, the river running down the middle, eight hundred feet below. There's an altercation, bad guy whips out a knife, slices the other guy, realizes how bad it is, throws both the vic and the knife over the edge."

"After going to the trouble to remove his coat?"

"Doesn't seem likely, does it?" He turned back onto the highway and headed south toward the New Mexico border. "Maybe Padilla is right—we just don't have the manpower to follow up on this. It would take a dozen searchers to comb the area under the bridge, and a little knife might never be found. Assuming it was thrown over that bridge. There are a zillion places to get rid of a small weapon like that."

"But a man was murdered. You can't simply let it go," Sam said. "Doesn't he have relatives, someone who would keep pushing at the Sheriff to get this solved?"

"We didn't find any next of kin. Sam, I'm not going to give up on this, even though the case is getting colder by the day. I'll get another warrant for Fenton's office and home, go through everything more closely if I can get some additional manpower. But I really doubt that's going to happen until Padilla is feeling securely re-elected."

Sam fumed over it for the next fifty miles but didn't come to any better conclusion, herself.

"I'd say it's safe for you to go back to the Adams place and do the rest of your cleanup, whenever you want," Beau told her as he dropped her off at her house.

At least it appeared that Cheryl Adams was alive, unharmed, and in the clear, and Sam felt relieved about that.

She stood in her driveway as Beau pulled away, debating whether to devote the remaining half-day to the cleanup or to get back to Sweet's Sweets and see how things were going there. A big head-slap later she was on her way to the bakery. What was she thinking, leaving her brand new business in the hands of two even-newer employees?

Her concern turned out to be for nothing. Jen was wiping tables that had obviously been filled with customers shortly before, and the half-empty cases attested to strong sales all morning. Becky had, per Sam's instructions, mixed and baked the sheets and layers for the big gala cake. All were cooling on the work table when she walked in. Sam would apply the 'dirty icing' and get them into the fridge this afternoon. Tomorrow she would assemble and decorate her masterpiece.

She showed Becky how to make small shrubs and pine trees out of sugar cones, modeling chocolate and royal icing.

"This is fun," Becky said after a couple of aborted attempts and then discovering the secret of holding the pastry bag at the correct angle.

"You're showing a natural knack for it. I'll show you some of the other techniques soon."

Sam decorated more Halloween cookies and told Jennifer how she wanted them arranged in the front windows—might as well pull in all the holiday business she could get. Her mind raced forward to Thanksgiving and then Christmas, knowing that unique pastries and plenty of variety in her made-from-scratch recipes would be what set her apart from the mundane offerings in the supermarkets. This first holiday season could very well get the business launched for all time.

"Will this be enough shrubs?" Becky asked from her end of the work table.

Sam glanced up to see about two dozen little bushes. "I think so. We'll probably only use eighteen or twenty of them, but it's always good to have extras in case of breakage."

"Got it." The two women lifted the board with the heavy sheet cake and carefully carried it into the walk-in fridge.

"Thank goodness for this thing," Sam said as she closed the door. "Would you believe that I used to have to bake all my sheet cakes in quarters and store them in a normal-sized fridge until the day of assembly. Then I'd put the whole thing together and get it delivered as fast as I could."

"You're loving the bakery, aren't you?" Becky commented.

Both phone lines rang at once. "I'll get one," shouted Jen. "Can you get two?"

"Yep, loving it," Sam said.

She picked up the second line and listened as the customer requested a special dessert for a family dinner on Sunday. Sam suggested an apple-pear tart that she'd recently tested at home. Seasonal fruit, easy to bake large enough for any number of people.

She'd no sooner hung up from taking that order than her cell phone buzzed inside her pocket.

"How are you doing with the property I gave you last week?" Delbert Crow asked. "Can we get real estate agents in there soon?"

She hedged and asked for another week. If she could just get her gala party done and those special orders for the election, she could budget an entire day for the Adams house.

Five o'clock. Jen closed out the register, handing Sam the tape showing the total and a bank bag with the cash, before leaving for the day. Becky had already gone, needing to be home for her kids.

Sam moved the few cookies and cupcakes from the window displays to the glass cases, covered the remaining product with clean white towels to keep them fresh, and turned out the lights in the front. In the kitchen she washed a couple of mixing bowls that hadn't been done earlier.

Outside, it was nearly dark. She called home and found that Kelly was already there.

"If you haven't started anything yet, I'll bring dinner home with me," Sam said.

"Pizza? I'll call it in." Kelly was a confirmed pizza-holic so the request came as no surprise. Sam could even guess what would be on it—everything. The large supreme pizza wouldn't do a lot for her own dieting plans, but then running a bakery wasn't exactly helping in that department either.

Thinking of food addictions reminded her that the weekly meeting of the book group, Chocoholics Unanimous, was coming up again soon. Last week, she had been so busy with the store opening that she'd only supplied them with some hastily baked cookies. This week she should strive for something more dramatic but at the moment she was fresh out of ideas.

Sam mulled over the idea of getting some help with her caretaking properties as she drove to Kelly's favorite pizza place, paid for their order and headed home. She'd thought of asking Kelly, but with Beau working so many extra hours these days, her daughter was tied up caring for his mother. Sam couldn't ask either of them to cut back on Iris's supervision. She'd already borrowed Darryl's crew several times, plus paying their rates would quickly eat up any income from the property. Mowing and trimming flowerbeds didn't quite fall into the same category as the heavy lifting that she physically couldn't do herself. She'd just have to make time for everything.

Sam found herself almost nodding off at the dinner table. She nibbled her way through one slice of the thick pizza. At least sleeping through meals would help her keep her diet on track, she thought.

"Mom, you're pooped! You should just go to bed early."

"Probably. But there's so much to do." She yawned. "At least I better get the menu finalized for the gala. We're doing a lot of free samples all day."

She told Kelly about the plan for the cake that replicated the shop. "If Beau can't get away to bring Iris to the party, will you do it?"

"Absolutely. I've been telling her about it and she's so excited. She wouldn't stay away on a bet."

"Good. Now, if I can just find the energy to get to the grocery store tonight for the special ingredients it'll be that much less I have to do tomorrow." She reached for a pen and notepad and began writing the list from memory. Cheeses, herbs, wines. Her head nodded but she kept writing. "Okay," she said finally.

"Mom, I'm not letting you drive anywhere tonight. You'd probably fall asleep, even though it's only a few blocks to the store." Kelly held out her hand. "Here. List." She wiggled her fingers.

Sam reluctantly pushed the page toward her daughter. "Okay. Just choose some decent wines."

"I can handle it."

Sam hardly remembered getting ready for bed. She rolled over and yawned the moment the bedroom lamp was out.

Chapter 14

Grocery bags waited on the kitchen table and Sam rummaged through them to be sure Kelly had found everything on her list. She scribbled a quick thank-you note and carried the bags out to the van.

The shop was quiet when she arrived and the clock told her it was still an hour or so before Jen and Becky would arrive. Sam got the first batches of breakfast pastries into the ovens before she took a break and found her coffee mug. The dark brew brought her out of the last of her morning fog. Each day got a little better, but Sam still wasn't sure how she—the original late sleeper—functioned before sunrise.

She was in the process of organizing ingredients for the savory treats for the party, matching them with the recipes to keep everything straight, when the phone rang.

Uh-oh, this can't be good, she thought as she reached

for it. Any call before six a.m. had to be bad news.

"Samantha Sweet," she said.

"Is this, um, the bakery—Sweet's Sweets?" a female voice asked. Assured that it was, she continued. "Elena Tafoya gave me your number. I'm in a bit of a bind, I'm afraid. I'm holding a little political fundraiser for our Senate candidate and need a dinner catered for thirty. It's this coming Sunday night."

Thanks a lot, Elena. Sam backed up against a storage shelf, hoping she hadn't actually said the words aloud. "We're just a pastry shop," was what she said, "not at all set up for dinner catering."

"I know, I'm sorry I didn't explain myself better. Elena thought you might know someone who caters. She said you have a friend who does breakfasts?"

Zoë? Sheesh. Asking her to make dinner for thirty people was a pretty far stretch from breakfast burritos for a dozen at the B&B. Plus, they were closed for the off season right now, not planning to start up again until skiers began to arrive in December.

"I'm afraid I can't—"

"Please hear me out. This is very important. The candidate gave us very little notice and the other place, uh, well, the dinner party will be held in my home. I can even provide staff to serve. I only need the food and desserts delivered sometime on Sunday."

Only. Why was it that people who wanted a huge favor usually thought of it as *only* one little thing?

"I'll pay double your usual rate." The voice was getting desperate.

Sam took a deep breath. "Let me check on it. Now, tell me a little more about what you had in mind for the food and for the desserts." *Why am I even talking to her? The week was crazy enough without this.*

She hung up the phone and looked at the clock. Zoë would normally be awake by now, getting her contractor husband off to his job. During the summer months she was easily up, with coffee brewing and something in the oven for her early-riser guests. Sam decided to take a chance.

"Sam? Everything okay?" Zoë sounded concerned, as she might well be under normal circumstances.

Sam gave her the gist of the desperate woman's phone call. "I got the feeling that some caterer backed out on her at the last minute. I don't know. Anyway, I talked her into a decorated cake for dessert. I should be able to feed thirty with a half-sheet. But I didn't have a clue what you could do for dinner, *if* you even want to do this."

"Well, things are slow now and I could use the extra money, with the B&B closed. How about Mexican food? Something different from the rubber chicken circuit that these politicians usually get, something I can make up in advance and deliver pretty easily?"

"I'll let you work that out with her. And make sure you let her know that I told you about the double-your-normal-price offer. Now that she's got us hooked, don't let her back out."

Zoë laughed. "Will do. I'll keep you posted."

Sam mixed up the batter for the half-sheet and was just pouring it into the pans when Becky came in.

"Hey there," she said. "Hard at it already?"

"You wouldn't believe. Can you get this into the oven and set the timer? Then maybe I can teach you how to make roses?"

While the cake baked, Sam whipped up some buttercream

frosting and tinted it in the candidate's colors. She pulled out decorating tips and wide-topped flower nails and had Becky follow along as she demonstrated how to form a small center cone, then add the petals in rows, building until the full-blown rose was finished. Becky botched a few but they got progressively better until she had a few keepers.

"Stay with it. If you mess one up, just scrape the icing back into the bowl. Put the good ones on this baking sheet and we'll refrigerate them so they set up firm."

While Becky continued making flowers, Sam piped out dozens of miniature versions of her butter cookies, which they would hand out as samples during the day Saturday. With the gala opening spanning the entire day, she had to think of things to make it special. Her signature blend coffee would be free all day, plus the sample-sized cookies and mini cupcakes. By happy hour they would switch to wine, with cheese and herb nibbles. And the gala cake shaped like the store would come out in the evening, to be served with a selection of coffees, teas, chai, and a hot mulled cider.

Her ads were due to start on the radio today and run every hour for two days. That, plus the editor of the newspaper had promised to send someone out to take photos and do a little write-up for the business section. If all that didn't bring the people in, she didn't know what would.

Beau called at some point but when Jen poked her head into the kitchen to tell Sam, her boss was putting some very delicate touches on the gala cake. Jen told Beau that Sam would have to call back, then tucked a message slip near the extension phone before dashing back to the front as the door chimes sounded.

By that evening, the two younger women had hung fairy

lights and set fresh flowers on all the tables, making sure there were plenty of coffee cups ready and that the display cases were full.

"Get a little extra rest," Sam told them before they left. "Tomorrow's going to be a long day."

"But worth it," Jen said. "Look how beautiful everything looks."

Sam had to agree. The shop had become everything she wanted it to be. She carried that thought with her, all the way home and up to the moment she crashed into bed. She'd completely forgotten to return Beau's call.

At five o'clock on Saturday they switched out the daytime overhead lights and Jen plugged in the strands of tiny white lights they had strung around the walls of the store. It gave the whole place a feeling of intimacy, with a party flair. The gala cake, the reproduction of the shop itself, sat near the front windows—clearly the showpiece of the party.

While Sam greeted her guests, Becky poured wine and Jen offered platters of miniature cheese biscuits, flaky herb twists and elegant hors d'oeuvres fashioned from their signature items.

The first to arrive were Ivan from Mysterious Happenings and Riki from Puppy Chic.

"Is *tres magnifique!*" Ivan exclaimed, taking the first glass of wine. "Your shop, she is the topping of neighborhood."

Sam thought something must have been lost in translation, but understood the sentiment. She gave him a hug.

"Samantha, it's just brilliant!" Riki stood near the gala cake, pointing and exclaiming over the details. "I must have you do one for my shop sometime."

Before Sam could thank her for the compliment, she saw Beau's Explorer outside. Kelly was climbing out of the backseat and the two of them brought out Iris's chair and helped her into it.

"I'm so glad you made it!" Sam said, bending to give Beau's mother a kiss on the cheek.

"Wouldn't miss it for anything," the white-haired lady said, wheeling herself toward the gala cake. "The shop looks positively magical!"

Beau slipped an arm around Sam's waist and kissed her ear. "Kelly explained about how busy you've been. The call wasn't that important anyway."

"Oh, Beau, last night! I totally forgot!"

"Don't you worry. Have a good time tonight and we'll talk tomorrow."

She started to give him a kiss but the door opened again, bringing a chill breeze and more guests. Elena looked elegant as ever in a turquoise silk blouse and skirt with a multicolored woven scarf—surely cashmere—draped over one shoulder. Sam recognized the man beside her as the former mayor, now running for governor.

"Sam, have you met my husband?"

Carlos Tafoya did the politician's handshake. Automatic smile, strong eye contact, his left hand cupping her elbow. Sam felt herself pulling back a fraction of a second before he let go. A dark feeling touched her, then was gone in a flash. Well, who wouldn't get a touch of the creeps from a politician?

Two of the Tafoya entourage introduced themselves: Martin Delgado, the campaign manager, and Kevin Calendar, a young campaign volunteer. Sam noted the dark suits and red ties that were *de rigueur* in the politico dress code.

"Carlos can't stay long," Elena was saying. "He has a speech in Albuquerque and a stop in Santa Fe. I just wanted him to see what a great job you've done with the shop." She turned to her husband, whose gaze had zipped around the room just short of the speed of light. "Isn't it a lovely place, darling?"

"Nice," he murmured.

"A real asset to the town, don't you think? Did I tell you that Sam makes absolutely everything from scratch. No mixes, nothing pre-made?"

He took a cheese twist from the platter Jen offered, but Sam noticed that he was paying more attention to Jen's behind as she moved on. "Uh, oh yes. You've done a great job with your place, Ms. Sweet." He munched the flaky pastry down in one bite, then moved around the room to shake hands and introduce himself to the dozen or more people who'd arrived since he came in. He quickly tired of that and after circling the room once, stepped over to Sam and thanked her for the invitation, wished her well with the business.

"I'll see you later," he said to Elena. Clearly his other event was a wives-not-included type.

Elena dropped her scarf across a chair and accepted a glass of wine from Becky. When Beau stopped by to tell Sam that he ought to be taking his mother home, she noticed that Elena excused herself to get another glass of wine.

The Cardwells said their goodbyes after awhile. Kelly offered to stay and help with the party if Sam would give her a ride out to Beau's place to retrieve her car later.

"That's okay, hon. We're doing fine here, and Beau can probably use your help with Iris. I'll see you at home later."

Orlando Padilla and his wife walked in about a minute after Beau drove away. Sam remembered being introduced to Margaret Padilla at another event recently. The sheriff's wife was attractive in a matronly way. Although Padilla was in his early fifties, and she assumed Margaret was as well, the wife dressed and acted older. Maybe just the traditional Spanish influence, Sam thought, smiling and shaking hands with both of them.

"Help yourselves to whatever you'd like. Coffee is set up on the back table, and there's tea or wine. We'll be cutting the cake about seven."

Padilla gave Sam that same politician's smile. "We can't stay too long. This time of year . . . well, you know next Tuesday is a pretty important day."

Sam nodded and wished him well. At that moment the reporter from the newspaper showed up and Sam went to greet her. The college-aged girl asked a few questions about the business and snapped several pictures of the displays and, finally, the gala cake.

"Can we get a shot of you cutting the cake and serving it to someone?"

Sam stepped to the cake table and posed making the first cut. As she placed the slice on a plate, Orlando Padilla stepped forward to receive it and smile for the camera. His grandstanding would have been especially funny, Sam thought, if Carlos Tafoya had stayed around. The two men would have probably started an elbow battle in order to get in the newspaper's photo. Padilla and his wife left a couple of minutes later.

Sam served several more slices of the cake. By now the room was full; probably at least fifty people were here. She looked around the room but didn't see Elena. Her beautiful scarf was still draped over the chair, though.

Sam turned the cake service over to Becky while she walked to the back to check the supply of coffee and teas. The hot mulled cider seemed to be going well.

Just then Elena came out of the back room. "Visited your little-girl's room. I hope you don't mind?"

"Of course not. Everything okay?"

Elena's smile seemed tight. "Just peachy."

Something wasn't right and Sam put a hand on Elena's arm. "It's crazy here right now but if you want to hang around awhile . . . maybe we could talk?"

Elena nodded. "I really don't want to go home alone right now."

"Stay then. How about some coffee and cake?"

Elena held up her wine glass. "I think I'll just top this off. I'll be fine. Get back to your guests."

By seven, the crowd had thinned considerably and when the last of the guests left at seven-thirty, Sam suggested that Jen and Becky go home too. "It's been a long day. I'll put a few things away, and then we can do a real clean-up tomorrow." Elena was the only one left.

"Whew! What a day," Sam said, settling into the chair across from Elena with a cup of hot chai. "I'm so glad we had a good turnout for the party."

"It was lovely, Sam, really, such a beautiful evening." Tears glistened in Elena's eyes.

Too much wine for you, girl. Sam eyed the other woman's half-empty glass. "Let me get you some tea. That cinnamon-orange one was really nice. Or cake. Did you get any of the cake?"

Elena's blond hair hung limply to her shoulders. "It's okay, Sam. I'm not really in the mood for cake."

"You do look pretty tired. I imagine the pace of the campaign is catching up. Bet you'll be glad when it's over, huh."

Elena picked up her glass and drained it in one gulp, then stood up and started unsteadily for the beverage table. Sam started to follow but sat down again. None of her suggestions had taken hold so far. At this point all she could do was insist on driving Elena home. She touched her friend's handbag, which was lying on the table. While Elena poured herself more wine, Sam lifted the clasp and slid her keys out, closing the bag and pocketing the keys before the other woman noticed.

"Oh, Sam, it's been . . . so . . . I can't explain it. You can't imagine."

Sam made some there-there noises, assurances that it would be over soon and life could settle into a new normality.

Elena set her glass on the table with a rattle. She paced to the front door and back, then sat down heavily, as if all the bones in her body had just withered.

"Sam, this will never be over. I have a terrible secret that will never go away."

Sam had a sudden vision of blood. The hairs on her neck rose.

"What, Elena? Who died?"

"I didn't say—" Her face had gone ghostly pale.

Sam stared at her, trying to piece together her own

forceful vision and Elena's reaction. As she watched, her friend's face crumpled into agony.

"I've killed a man, Sam."

Chapter 15

Sam gave a halfhearted heh-heh chuckle. Then she caught Elena's expression. "You're serious?" Her blood rushed through her veins. Her hands, cupped around the mug of hot chai, felt icy. "Elena? What are you saying?"

Tears flowed down Elena's face and her nose was running. Sam unconsciously grabbed for a paper napkin and handed it to her.

"I did it. I didn't mean to, but I killed him."

"Slow down. Who do you think you killed.?" Sam could not wrap her mind around the idea of her elegant friend killing anyone, not even accidentally.

Elena balled up the paper napkin, kneading it with fingers that could not stay still. "Carlos has become so cold, so distant to me. His career is everything. I just felt so . . . ugly. Like he doesn't want me anymore."

Sam struggled to comprehend what Elena was saying.

"I started seeing another man. I don't know why." A sob ripped out of her. "It was stupid. Carlos became suspicious. I had to be so careful, but I couldn't stop seeing this man."

"You killed your lover?"

"No, it was a stranger. I'd been with my lover. I was walking to where I'd parked my car. The footsteps . . . someone was following me. I got so scared. I thought . . . well, it was dark and not the best part of town. I could only think of protecting myself and I had this little knife in my purse and I just thought that maybe if he saw it he would back away. I slashed at him but I didn't know it would—" She choked and dissolved in tears. "The man was grabbing at his neck, holding the collar of his coat up to it . . . I think he tried to yell. I don't know."

Bram Fenton. No wonder the investigator's notes were encrypted. Among his clients had been the former mayor.

Then Sam remembered the trench coat. The picture confused her—where was Elena's car parked? Where did the knife incident take place? "Did he follow you out to the gorge bridge?" Sam asked.

Elena's sob turned into a hiccup and she stared at Sam. "No . . . why would you think that?"

"Never mind. What did you do next?"

Elena took a breath, blew her nose on the napkin. "I panicked. All I could think of was getting away . . . I ran."

Tears continued to run down Elena's cheeks and she looked drained.

"Elena, you need to tell the authorities about this. I'm sure they'll see that it was self-defense. An accident that the cut was fatal."

Her red-rimmed eyes went wide. "No! Sam, that's not an option. I—Carlos—the election is everything to him. He would—"

She reached for her purse and scarf. "I have to get going."

"Elena, calm down. We'll give it some thought. Meanwhile, you're not driving. You've had a lot to drink and you are way too upset." Sam pulled Elena's keys from her pocket. "I'll drive you home and give these back to you when we get there. You can come back for your car tomorrow."

Elena looked like she wanted to argue the point but she submitted. She gave Sam her address.

During the drive, Elena sat slumped in the passenger seat. The ordeal of telling her awful secret had clearly drained every ounce of her energy. Sam concentrated on the drive, on getting Elena into her house. Her mind couldn't yet wrap itself around the deed and the implications for her friend.

"Please don't tell Deputy Cardwell," Elena whispered to Sam. "It won't solve anything."

"Get some sleep," Sam said. "We'll decide what to do, later."

Fine advice Sam thought as she fought for sleep, hours later. Elena, a killer? The woman's distraught face appeared to Sam at every turn. She would roll over in bed, there would be Elena. She puzzled over the logistics. Elena, walking toward her car parked on a side street in town. It must have been fairly near one of the hotels. Nowhere near the isolated gorge bridge, miles outside town on the west side. The only question with an answer was the part about how Fenton's trench coat had become saturated with his blood. But how had that coat ended up in Cheryl Adams's closet? Did Cheryl and Elena know each other? The elegant mayor's wife, acquaintance of the young trailer park mother? If Cheryl Adams had offered to hide the bloody evidence, she'd certainly pulled a good bluff on Beau when they interviewed her.

Sam rolled over in bed for the hundredth time, wrestling with the dilemma about how much to tell Beau versus leaving it up to Elena. When she looked at her bedside clock, it showed four-fifty in the morning and she didn't feel like she'd had a wink of sleep.

I could at least be doing something *with my time*, she decided, fumbling about in the dark room for some clothes. The mess from the party still needed to be dealt with, and even though Sweet's Sweets would be closed today, Sunday, there was plenty of work to be done.

By nine o'clock Sam had managed to put much of last night's drama behind her. Amazing what a few hours of vigorous cleaning will do for an unsettled mind. She'd tossed out the scraps of snacks, which didn't look nearly as appetizing in the pre-dawn as they had last night, trashed paper plates and plastic wine glasses, washed platters and coffee makers and reassembled the remains of the gala cake—the square tier replica of the shop itself—presenting it on a fresh cake board and putting it on display in the front window.

The half-sheet cake for tonight's catered dinner was simple to whip up and she felt herself relaxing as the scent filled the bakery. Mopping floors to the accompaniment of warm cake batter offered a soothing respite. After stashing the cleaning gear and decorating the sheetcake, Sam headed home.

"Hey, Mom." Kelly was busy in the kitchen. "How about if I make us a nice breakfast in honor of the first time we've both had a day off in ages? Eggs benedict?"

"I'd love that," Sam said. "Is there time for me to grab a quick shower?"

She emerged from the steamy bathroom ten minutes later, cogitating on the idea of eating Kelly's nice breakfast and then sleeping the day away. She could do it as long as she awoke in time to deliver the cake for the senate candidate's dinner that night.

"Nearly ready," Kelly said. Eighties music came from the radio on the counter and she swayed in time to it as she topped the poached eggs with hollandaise sauce.

Sam found silverware and napkins and hastily set the table. Aside from two pilfered cookies at her shop, she'd eaten nothing since the previous night—and very little then. Thinking of the evening brought back her dilemma about how much of Elena's confession to tell Beau.

"Here we go," Kelly said, setting their plates on the table and pulling out her chair. Belatedly, she remembered the salt and pepper and as she was rising to get them, the music stopped and the voice of the news announcer came on.

Sam paid little attention until a familiar name grabbed her. ". . . Elena Tafoya, wife of the former mayor and gubernatorial candidate Carlos Tafoya, found dead in the couple's home this morning, an apparent suicide."

Her fork dropped with a clatter. She felt the blood drain from her face.

"Mom? What's the matter?" Kelly mumbled through a mouthful of egg.

"Shh, I need to hear this." Sam leaned toward the radio, but the announcer had already gone on to other stories.

"No, no, no . . . I can't believe it—"

"What, Mom?" Kelly had set aside her own fork and was staring at Sam.

"Elena—I think you met her last night. Pretty blond, wearing a turquoise silk blouse . . . the wife of Carlos Tafoya. They just said that she's died."

"Mom, ohmygod, how awful."

Sam's head buzzed, like a swarm of insects drilling at her brain with a terrible drone. Impossible. She'd just seen Elena, just talked with her. She'd been upset but not suicidal. Surely not. There had to be a mistake.

The ringing in her head began to coalesce, and Sam realized it was the phone. Kelly had already jumped up to answer it.

"We just heard," she was saying.

Sam waited, numb, not wanting to talk to anyone.

"Sure. No problem. Twenty minutes? You're sure?" Kelly's side of the conversation made no sense until she handed the phone out to Sam.

"It's Beau," she told her mother. "He's been called out to the Tafoya's home and wants to know if I can come over and stay with Iris. I told him I would. Now he wants to speak with you."

He gave her the bare facts—yes, it was true that Elena was dead. Until he got to the scene he wouldn't know for sure, but the call indicated that she'd hung herself with a long piece of woven material.

"Beau, I need to talk to you about this. Can you call me the minute you are finished at the scene?"

"What do you know, Sam?"

What *did* she know? Nothing, really. And everything. At least protecting Elena's privacy over the affair and the death of Bram Fenton were no longer a priority. It was all bound to come out now. "I don't think she killed herself," Sam told Beau.

"Darlin, everyone feels that way when it's a friend or relative. It's just so hard to accept. Eventually you'll get used to the idea."

"Elena and I had a long talk last night, after the rest of the guests left the shop. I need to tell you about it."

"Okay . . ." The word dragged out as he considered the possibilities. "I can't let you near the scene."

"I couldn't handle it."

"Good. I mean, it's good that you aren't going to fight me on that. I'll call you when I can get away."

"Beau? Take good care of her. She was just so—" Sam choked on a sob.

"I will, sweetheart. Don't worry." She hung onto the phone long after his call clicked off and the dial tone began buzzing in her ear.

Kelly hurriedly jammed down a few more bites of her breakfast. "Sorry that I need to leave so fast," she said. "Would you like to come with me out to the Cardwell's? It might be better if you didn't stay here alone."

Sam took a deep breath and forced a weak smile. "No, no, I'll be fine. I could really use some sleep."

She watched as Kelly grabbed up her jacket and purse, and stood leaning against the kitchen counter as her daughter's red car pulled out of the long driveway.

Sleep. Like that would be possible.

Her brain swirled with a million thoughts, reliving last night's conversation, seeing Elena with her multicolored scarf around her shoulders. The secret she revealed was a terrible one, granted. But Fenton's dying had been an accident, Elena's strike against him she believed to be self defense. Sam tried to remember what she'd said to her friend, how they'd left things. Elena's state of mind—frightened, worried, secretive. She clearly didn't want her husband to know the truth. But was she scared enough to kill herself?

A chill settled over Sam and didn't go away even when she crawled back under the thick quilts on her bed. She'd insisted that Elena go to the authorities.

And that, she feared, was the thing that pushed the poor woman over the edge.

Chapter 16

The bedroom was dim with late afternoon light when Sam awoke with a start. Despite her whirling thoughts and ragged emotions, exhaustion won out and she'd drifted off to sleep for several hours. She stared at the clock, uncomprehending, until it hit her that the thing she had to remember was to deliver the cake for the Senator's dinner, which started at six.

She dragged herself to the bathroom and splashed cold water on her face, combing her hair into a semblance of order and then wandering back to her closet for fresh clothes. Thank goodness she didn't have to play hostess tonight. No way she could have handled that. She checked her appearance in the mirror; with puffy eyes and ghostlike skin she was barely presentable.

She'd obviously slept more soundly than she imagined. In the kitchen three messages blinked on her machine:

one from Zoë asking whether they might want to drive to the party together to deliver the food and dessert; one from Kelly saying that she would be staying with Iris past dinnertime; the final one from Beau to inform her that they'd nearly finished processing the scene and that he'd try her cell. On the cell, he'd said that he would call her again when he actually got away. He could either come by her house or they could meet somewhere. When she returned Zoë's call, Darryl informed her that Zoë had already left. Sam erased the messages then got in the van and drove to the shop.

Sweet's Sweets was quiet, as was the street at this time of day. Most of the small retail businesses along here were closed on Sundays, one main reason that Sam had decided to take the day off as well. She pulled to the alley behind and went inside.

Wrestling the large cake board from the walk-in fridge, she admired her handiwork. *Good thing I did this one before I learned about Elena—my hands wouldn't have been nearly this steady,* she thought. She felt the telltale prickle of tears again and forced herself to think of something else. Reviewing the directions to the hostess's home, she secured the cake in the back of the van and started out.

The large house sat perched on a steep hillside with views of the town, the river and the far-off volcanoes in the west. The sun was well below the horizon, leaving the sky in brilliant crimson, as Sam followed the winding drive.

Guest cars filled two pullout areas and she bypassed them, hoping there was a separate service entrance. When she spotted Zoë's little Subaru wagon, she headed that direction.

The kitchen bustled with activity. A housekeeper seemed

to be in charge, a thin reed of a woman who was speaking urgently with a lady in full Taoseña regalia, brushed silk skirt and top with loads of turquoise jewelry.

"Ah, the cake," the dressy lady said. "We were beginning to worry." She said it in a tone that really meant 'it's about time.' She turned her back and left it to the housekeeper to organize and instruct Sam where to put it.

"The cake can go on that table," the other woman said. She, too, turned around and began directing others. Sam spotted Zoë in a corner of the large kitchen, checking something under foil in a large chafing dish. She gave a quick nod toward her friend and headed out to the van to get the cake.

"Now I know why I don't often cater meals for rich people," Zoë said as they walked out to their vehicles together after assuring that the serving staff were ready to handle the actual interaction with guests. "Too many bosses and too many opinions."

Zoë had grown up in a hippie commune in the sixties where food consisted of whatever someone cooked at whatever time they cooked it. No whining unless you wanted to do it yourself.

"So, what's up with you? You were beaming all over last night, and now you look like something that's been run over and left by the road." Zoë looked at her suspiciously. "Have a little *too* much fun last night?"

"Not that kind," Sam assured her. "I just found out this morning that a friend died." She still had a hard time saying the words.

"Oh, god, Sam. I'm sorry. I shouldn't have been so flippant."

"It's okay. You didn't know."

"Come home with me. We're having the same dinner as all these snooty political donors, minus the speeches and the groveling. I made extra." Zoë took Sam's hand and squeezed it. "You look like you shouldn't be alone tonight."

Sam hesitated. Being alone probably wasn't the best thing for her, but she couldn't imagine coming up with dinner conversation either. "I, uh—" Her cell buzzed inside her pocket and she pulled it out to look. "It's Beau. I, um, I may have some information about his current case and he wants to talk to me."

"If you didn't look as if you were about to go to a dental appointment, I'd think that was just an excuse to see Mr. Gorgeous." She gave a half wink. "Go—get the interview done. If you want to talk later, I'll be home."

Sam caught the call just before it went to voice mail, and she waved bye to Zoë.

"Hey there. Glad I caught you," Beau said.

"Yeah, sorry I managed to sleep through all the other messages."

"You needed the rest. So. I need to hear about this final conversation between you and Elena Tafoya. Is it something that needs to be done at my office, with a stenographer and all?"

Sam hadn't considered that. She fumbled an answer.

"How about if we meet somewhere private. You tell me about it. If it's the kind of thing that needs to go into the record we'll re-do it, officially."

"Thank you. I . . . I guess I'm . . ."

"Still shaken up. I know. Since Kelly's at my house with Mama, how about if I come to your place? Have you eaten?"

Less than a bite of egg at breakfast, Sam realized. Nothing since. "I don't feel hungry."

"By that answer, I'm guessing you've had nothing all day. I can't have you wasting away to nothing. I'll bring a bucket of chicken."

Wasting away to nothing was not going to happen in this century, Sam thought, but it was nice of him to offer. They agreed to meet at her house in thirty minutes.

Beau was sensitive enough not to bring up the subject of Elena's death right away. Despite believing she couldn't eat a bite, the smell of the spicy chicken captured Sam and she surprised herself by eating three pieces, along with coleslaw and a biscuit.

"I'll never lose these extra pounds if you keep treating me this way," she told Beau as they cleared the paper plates away and put coffee on to brew.

"Have I ever asked you to? I've told you, I like you just the way you are." He pulled her close and she tried to relax against him. But the upcoming conversation was eating at her.

"Let's take our coffee into the living room and sit down. This may take awhile."

Suddenly she felt nervous about what she knew. But she laid it all out, everything Elena had said about her affair and how someone was following her down a dark street. The knife, the blood. How she'd run away as the man gripped at the collar of his coat.

"Don't you see? It was Bram Fenton," Sam said. "Carlos Tafoya must have been his last client, the man who hired him to watch Elena and catch her in the affair."

"She mentioned the trench coat?"

"She said he held his coat collar against his neck, where the knife caught him."

"But she left him on the street, nowhere near the gorge bridge?"

"I mentioned the gorge and she was really puzzled. She wasn't out there."

Beau stood up and paced to the far end of the room. "So how did Bram Fenton end up at the bottom of the gorge? Someone took the coat off him and moved the body."

"Cheryl Adams? The coat was at her house."

"You saw her, Sam. She's about ninety pounds soaking wet. How'd she pick up a lifeless man and move him? Much less get him up and over the railing on the bridge?"

"With help?"

His eyes squinted nearly closed as he thought about it. "I don't know. I sure didn't get the feeling she knew anything about Fenton or his coat."

Sam sipped at her coffee but it tasted bitter in her mouth. "Even though she admitted to the killing, I couldn't help but feel sorry for Elena in all this. After she told me the story, I suggested that she needed to report it. That the case was surely self defense. She got panicky when I told her that."

She set the nearly full mug on an end table. "Beau, I feel like I might have pushed her too hard. Maybe she was so scared that—"

"Sam, you can't start thinking that way. You did not make Elena Tafoya kill herself." He sat beside her on the sofa and put an arm around her shoulders. "She admitted that she was really unhappy in her marriage. That was the whole reason for the affair, right?"

She nodded against his shoulder.

"She might have done this anyway, even if she'd never talked to you about it." He kissed her hair. Then her temple. Then her mouth.

After his kisses had worked their magic for a few more minutes they found themselves in the bedroom, and an hour later Sam felt a lot better. She snuggled against his solid chest, wishing he could stay right in this spot all night. But it was not to be.

"Poor Kelly," he said after awhile. "She was supposed to get the day off. I'm sure she's got other things she'd rather do than care for an old woman."

"She loves Iris," Sam assured him. "I know my daughter. She wouldn't have taken the job if she wasn't happy to do it."

"But still . . ."

"Yeah, still. She probably *would* like to get out with some of her friends now and then."

Beau pulled himself away, leaving the warm quilt tucked around Sam. She stretched luxuriously and watched him put his uniform back on, admiring the way the fitted shirt hugged his shoulders, the way his jeans fit just right. She stifled that line of thinking before she could reach out and drag him back into her bed.

Grabbing a robe, Sam walked him to the back door and watched as his cruiser pulled away. As the languor of great sex began to fade, Sam found herself thinking about Elena again. She switched on the TV set in the living room and tucked herself into one corner of the sofa.

The nightly news was just coming on and, even on the Albuquerque channels, Elena's death was the top story.

Cameras focused on Carlos Tafoya and reporters gathered around him at the little impromptu news conference on the steps of the county courthouse. After a few of the usual absurd "how do you feel" questions, the press got to the meat of what they really wanted to know.

"Mr. Tafoya, does this mean that you'll be dropping out of the race?" "Do you feel that you can still serve in office at this point?"

Carlos looked solemnly out over the gathering, waiting for a pause in the rush of questions. "My beloved wife's death has deeply shaken our family. We are understandably distraught. But my entire life has been devoted to public service and I shall press on and continue with my duty. Pain subsides with time and I can make it through this. So, yes, my name will still be on the ballot next Tuesday."

In a display of utter bad taste, someone asked how soon the funeral services would take place. Less than eighteen hours after Elena's death—Sam cringed at the tactlessness.

Carlos had the good grace to duck his head and say that a private memorial would be scheduled.

Sam hoped to go, to honor Elena's memory. She could surely find out what the plans were from Beau. She flipped among the four local stations, wondering if there was any additional information but they all had identical film and no new questions.

When Kelly came in, Sam was nodding off.

"Mom, you okay?" Kelly leaned over the back of the couch and landed a gentle kiss on Sam's cheek.

"Yeah, I will be. Eventually." She groaned her way to her feet and switched off the TV. "I better be getting some sleep. The bakery opens pretty early in the morning."

It was hard to imagine getting back into a normal routine, but Sam moved on autopilot through her nightly ritual for bedtime.

When she arrived at Sweet's Sweets at five-thirty a.m. it was to find Jen and Becky already at work.

"We thought you might want to sleep a little late this morning," Jen said, taking a tray of cinnamon scones from the oven. She turned to slide three pans of muffins inside.

"I would have loved that," Sam said, "if I'd actually been sleeping."

"We heard about Mrs. Tafoya," Becky said. "It was so shocking, her just being at our party the night before."

"I took her home," Sam said. "I was worried that she'd had too much to drink and might have an accident."

Little did I know.

"Is it true, what they're saying on the news?" asked Jen. "That she killed herself?"

"I don't know. Deputy Cardwell is investigating. He seems to think that's what happened." Sam walked absentmindedly to the tray where she placed orders to be filled. "It's—well, it's complicated."

She caught a glance at their inquisitive faces. No way would she spread stories of Elena's troubles. "Okay, let's get this place organized. We need a chocolate creation for the Chocoholics group at the bookstore. Becky, can I turn that one over to you? Put your imagination to work, as long as everything on the dessert is chocolate."

She came to the order form she'd filled out for Elena's order—the victory cake for her husband's celebration. They'd first talked about it almost two weeks ago. Now, although everything had changed, it had also stayed the same. Carlos was still on the ballot, the election would take place in a few days . . . and Elena wouldn't be there. A tear dropped onto the sheet of paper.

Sam hastily wiped it away. She took a deep breath. Cleared her head. Elena had paid for the cake and it was up to Sam to deliver it. She filed the order form and sketches so she would come back to them the day before the election.

Sam took a look at the creation on which Becky was working, a chocolate headstone over a chocolate grave, complete with cookie-crumb dirt and a rising ghost of white chocolate.

"I hope it's—I didn't mean to be morbid," Becky said. "Mr. Petrenko said they're reading a ghost story this week, and with Halloween and all . . ."

"It's perfect," Sam said. "Business must go on, and I'm happy to see how well you've captured their theme. And I love the little sculpted spiders and bats. Great job."

She walked out to the sales floor, where Jen was doing a brisk business in breakfast pastries and coffee, the Monday crowd needing a little something extra to wake them up on the way to their jobs in nearby shops and offices. Sam recognized quite a few faces from the Saturday night gala, happy to see that people were returning.

The goodwill created by the party was definitely paying off. She mingled, said hello to several, made sure the coffee was plentiful and the plate of samples filled with variety. The phone had been ringing all morning and Jen clearly could use a break from it, as she waited on customers.

"I'll grab that in the back," Sam said, hurrying to the other extension. "Sweet's Sweets."

"Hi, darlin, it's me."

"Beau. Have you found out anything new?"

"One thing you might be interested in. There's a memorial for Elena tomorrow afternoon at the funeral home chapel. Carlos is skipping a church funeral mass and has arranged for cremation."

"Already?" Sam felt a rock fall to the pit of her stomach.

"Seems rushed to me, too. But with the election coming up . . . well, I don't know if he's just overwhelmed with things to do right now, or if he's trying to jump while the sympathy factor is high." He paused. "I'm sorry, that was not a kind thing to say."

"It might be true, though." Sam remembered her own uncharitable thoughts about whether she wanted to bake a victory cake for Carlos. "I don't know, Beau. I'm kind of numb about it. Guess I'm just moving through the day as best I can."

"I know. Look, maybe we could go together? There's a wake at his campaign manager's house after. At least he understood what poor taste it would be to invite people to the very rooms in which . . . it happened."

"Are we invited, to the wake?"

"I don't much care. I want to watch Carlos Tafoya in action, to see if I can judge the level of his grief. Because I have a real hinky feeling about this, especially with all the things Elena told you on her last night."

"I'll bake a memorial cake and we'll take it. They'd have a hard time turning us away."

Chapter 17

The pain was still too raw. It revealed itself on the faces of every person in the chapel. Elena's portrait depicted a calm and polished woman. It was the official, candidate's-wife shot that had been widely circulated along with Carlos's own photos during the campaign. The flowers were large and showy and impersonal. The actual cremation probably hadn't taken place yet, Beau told Sam, since the medical investigator's office only released the body this afternoon. It was just as well, she thought, that they didn't all have to stare at some metal urn up there.

Sam and Beau sat in the back row, the better to watch the crowd, he said. A law enforcement habit, she supposed. But why was he thinking along those lines?

From what Beau had told her about the circumstances of Elena's death, he'd concluded it had happened at her own hands. The office of the medical examiner agreed, finding elevated levels of alcohol and sleeping pills in her system, but not fatal amounts. Sam herself could attest to the amount of wine her friend had drunk. And after her shocking revelation about killing a man, it wouldn't come as a big surprise if she'd taken a little sleep aid before going to bed. But then she hadn't gone to bed.

Had she been depressed enough to end her life?

Sam couldn't quite rest easily with that theory.

The speaker's words droned on, a blur to Sam. Carlos Tafoya sat in the front pew beside his father, Sam's landlord, Victor Tafoya. The next several rows were reserved for family but most of the chapel seemed to be filled with Carlos's political entourage and a selection of the curious and morbid. Sam found herself hoping that no one thought that of her.

With no graveside service to end the observance, goodbyes were said in the form of a reception line at the front of the chapel. Sam noticed that Carlos handed some of the people a small card, presumably the address of the wake.

"I already know where it is," Beau whispered to her. "Go forward if you want, but I can skip this part."

Sam decided that she could, as well.

"I took the cake to my house," Sam told him as they left. "We need to stop by and pick it up on the way."

In her kitchen she handed Beau the half-sheet, decorated in white-on-white with Elena's portrait reproduced in edible color on top and touches of her favorite turquoise woven into the decorations.

"I'll be right there," she said. She went into her bedroom, slipped into more comfortable shoes and glanced at the wooden box.

The lumpy old thing, which had once seemed almost grotesque to her, warmed her with comfort when she picked it up. She hugged it to her and let her pain over Elena's death retreat. Like a tangible thing, the dark feeling left her heart, traveled down her arms, through her fingertips and—unbelievably—into the box. Sam held it out, balanced on the palms of her hands, and stared at it.

Elena, I will find out what happened, I promise.

The red stones winked back at her, brighter this time than their green and blue counterparts. Puzzled, Sam set the box on her dresser and backed out of the room.

"Everything okay?" Beau asked, reaching out to give her a hug.

"Yeah. I'll be fine." Actually, she felt better than fine. For the first time in days she had a feeling that everything would turn out all right. They would figure out what really happened to both Bram Fenton and Elena and how to set her spirit free.

They rode silently for a few minutes in Beau's Explorer, headed for the wake at the home of Carlos Tafoya's campaign manager. No one, it seemed, could face a visit to the house where Elena's death had happened, barely thirty-six hours earlier.

"You know, there's a lot about this that still bothers me," Sam said, finally. "Aside from the fact that I don't believe Elena killed herself over it."

Beau stared steadily at the road ahead. "It bothers me too. I've told Sheriff Padilla that we need to launch a more thorough search for the knife and I want a warrant to search Elena's possessions for clues, before Carlos clears out her stuff and moves into the governor's mansion."

"And?"

"And I have a feeling he's shuffled the request to the bottom of the stack."

"But why?" Sam had never especially warmed up to Beau's boss, the sheriff who seemed more show than substance.

"Politics? Well, everything's about politics this time of year. He's so overly conscious of getting re-elected right now . . . and it probably wouldn't be a good move for him to drag the Tafoya name through the mud right now either. If—I should say, when—Carlos Tafoya is elected governor, he'll have power to sign a lot of funding for the county. If we're ever to get our own crime lab, or even an extra assistant or two to help at crime scenes . . . well, the funding has to come from higher up."

"So you think that Padilla and Tafoya are buddies, kind of helping each other's campaigns, for that reason?"

He shrugged.

"Aren't there internal investigations for this sort of thing? To discover whether a law officer isn't playing by the rules?"

"I'll push harder for the warrant after the election. It's only a few more days. It's just that evidence can disappear or be tampered with . . . oh, hell, what am I saying? Fenton's death happened weeks ago. If something was going to vanish, it probably already did." He slowed as they reached the road they were looking for. "Plus, selfishly, I'll take a lot less flack from Padilla if I wait awhile. The guy's been jumping down everyone's throats recently. Pre-election PMS or something, I guess."

Sam snickered at the image of the squat Padilla storming

around the office like a wild woman on hormone overload.

"Control that grin of yours," Beau cautioned. "He's here."

Sure enough, Padilla's county car was parked among the dozen or so in front of the traditional adobe that sat overlooking the Rio Fernando from a bluff lined with brilliant yellow cottonwoods. Sam retrieved the cake from the back of Beau's vehicle and they walked through an entry gate, past plantings of flowers and shrubs that looked as if they received daily tending by a master gardener.

The first person they encountered, just inside the front door, was Orlando Padilla's wife, Margaret. She greeted them warmly and suggested that they place the cake on the dining table where a buffet of catered food interspersed with homemade dishes was set up.

"This is beautiful," Margaret said. "Such a nice tribute to Elena's memory." She moved a couple of casseroles around, making space for the cake. "I didn't know her very well, myself, but my husband says she was a classy lady."

"Yes, she was," Sam agreed. "I'd only recently gotten to know her."

The sheriff approached just then, greeting Beau and Sam in his offhand manner. He turned to his wife and steered her toward the kitchen. "Excuse us a minute," he said, almost as an afterthought.

Beau raised an eyebrow toward Sam. "See what I mean about his total self-absorption," he murmured.

Another couple came into the dining room just then; Beau took Sam's elbow and they turned toward the large living room where most of the crowd were standing around chatting in small groups. She recognized the publisher of the local newspaper and the wife of a town council member as two of the important people in the gathering. She also spotted Martin Delgado and Kevin Calendar from the Tafoya campaign among the guests. For the most part, it wasn't her usual social set at all.

The recent widower mingled with the guests. With friends he seemed to be genuinely grieving. But Sam noticed that with others he immediately went into a low-key version of campaign mode. She caught herself watching him, remembering things Elena had said—the difficulty of life in the limelight, the stresses her husband's career placed upon her. The affair. Sam felt her throat tighten. So sad. Maybe the lifestyle, as much as Elena's guilt over the affair and Fenton's death, had driven her to desperation.

Orlando and Margaret Padilla stepped into the room just then. Tafoya's voice trailed off momentarily and he stared toward the sheriff. Sam felt a hum begin in her ears. She pressed her fingertips to her temples. Beau had turned to speak to someone else. She glanced back toward Padilla who was intent on filling a plate. Tafoya's conversation had resumed and everyone seemed unaware of the strange current that Sam felt.

She shook her head and the hum faded away.

What was that all about?

Her arms were covered in goose bumps. Her scalp itched from them, as if her hair were standing on end. In a split second, the bumps disappeared and her hands felt on fire.

"Beau—" But he didn't hear her. She gave him a vague wave to indicate that she was going to step outside.

A set of French doors stood open to a patio, letting in the mild autumn afternoon. She edged her way through the crowded room and took a deep breath of chrysanthemum-scented air. A waist-high adobe wall enclosed the free-form flagstone patio, providing a safety barrier from the drop-off behind the house. Sam stood at the wall, soaking up the views of the ravine beyond, placing her hands against the cool mud surface.

"It was a little close in there, wasn't it?"

Sam's hand flew to her chest at the sound of the male voice behind her. Orlando Padilla stood less than three feet away, trying to stick a fork into an olive on his plate.

"Sam, isn't it?" he said. "Beau talks about you a lot."

She nodded, trying to force her heartbeat back to normal.

"Good man. I'm glad to have him in the department." Padilla continued speaking around a tortilla chip. "With the election and everything, life has been pretty busy these last few months."

She mumbled something in acknowledgment but couldn't concentrate on his words. A dark blue haze began to form around his head, snaking around him until it engulfed his shoulders and sent tendrils toward his feet.

"Are you feeling okay, Ms. Sweet?"

The blue deepened, turned muddy gray, became more solid-looking.

Sam's mouth opened, then closed again. Padilla's face was nearly obscured now.

"Sam? Ms. Sweet?"

The colored haze vanished as quickly as it had appeared. Sam blinked hard. *What on earth?*

"Hey you," Beau said, slipping an arm around Sam's waist. "I thought you'd gone missing."

She sent a vague smile his direction.

"What's up?" Beau asked, trying to keep it casual.

"I . . ."

Margaret Padilla called out from the doorway to let her husband know that they would be late if they didn't get going. She smiled apologetically. "Another day, another speech," she said.

Orlando Padilla gave Sam a long, hard stare. She squirmed just a little. Then he drew a deep breath and walked toward the house.

"What was that all about?" Beau asked.

"I had . . ." She wanted to tell him about the nearly-painful sound that had pierced her ears earlier and the bizarre colors that had appeared around Padilla, but something held her back. Until she had some clue what all the weird signals were about it was better to keep it to herself. "Nothing really. Maybe it's a migraine coming on."

Two women stepped outside, an older lady that Sam thought had been introduced as someone's aunt and a middle-aged woman in a deep burgundy dress with a delicate lace collar. Beau stood a little straighter and sent a polite nod their direction.

"Do you want to go home?" he asked.

She waved off the suggestion. "I'll be fine."

Another group had discovered the patio by now, Carlos Tafoya among them. Someone snagged Beau with a question and Sam let her attention wander. As her gaze drifted toward Tafoya, she felt her breath catch. Obscuring his handsome face and ready political smile was a blue haze.

Oh god, not another one.

She blinked hard and looked away, out to the open land beyond the adobe house. When she looked back at Tafoya the aura was gone.

Chapter 18

I can't help it, Beau. I got the weirdest feelings around both Carlos Tafoya and Orlando Padilla. I felt such tension in the room." It was the only explanation she could offer when he quizzed her about her reaction at the wake. They were in his SUV on their way downtown. Sam had asked Beau to drop her off at her shop so she could see how the girls had done without her there all afternoon.

"Did you get the feeling that Tafoya might have guessed about his wife's affair?"

"Maybe. But if he did, I don't think he confronted Elena. She would have told me."

She rubbed her temples, although she felt no pain. The whole thing was just so confusing.

"Dinner later?" he asked. "I put some stew in the cooker this morning. It'll be real easy."

"Would it be okay if I beg off? It was an early

morning."

He looked disappointed. "Tomorrow then? Stew is even better the next night."

She didn't have the heart to turn him down for the second invitation.

At Sweet's Sweets, Jen was in the process of closing out the register and Becky had gone home for the day, leaving a supply of tea cookies and cakes ready for sale the next day. Sam would come in early and get the breakfast pastries done in time for the early coffee crowd and Halloween cookies baked for the trick-or-treat promotion they'd been advertising. Two new custom orders had come in— a wedding cake for the end of the month (at least some customers planned ahead!) and a baby shower cake which reminded Sam that new life always came along to offer comfort over the loss of another.

She made up a quick sketch for a three-dimensional cake, a baby carriage surrounded by large toy blocks, all frosted in pastel buttercream, with a set of life-size yellow booties made of sugar. She could do the basics in the morning and put it all together the next day. She rechecked the window displays and left the night lights on before going out to her van, parked behind the shop.

Kelly's car sat in the driveway at home when Sam arrived.

"Beau came straight home after the funeral," Kelly said, "so I started dinner early. Hope that's okay."

"I'm not very hungry," Sam said. She had to admit, though, that when Kelly lifted the lid on a simmering skillet of chicken and mushrooms in some kind of savory sauce she might rethink that. "Okay, maybe just a little."

Kelly chatted while they ate, but Sam found her mind

wandering to Elena, specifically their last conversation. Granted, they'd consumed a fair amount of wine but Sam found herself racking her brain to remember anything at all that might have been her clue as to what Elena would do later that evening.

On the surface perhaps Elena did have reason to end her life. Her unhappy marriage, the disappointment of the affair, and the crime she'd committed—accidentally or not—all of it had eaten at her until she obviously could not bear it.

"I'm going to bed early," Sam told Kelly as they put the dishes into the dishwasher. The energy boost that she normally got from the wooden box seemed to have vanished after her experiences with the oddly colored auras and the piercing buzz in her head.

She summoned up enough energy to brush her teeth and slip into her nightshirt before crashing. Elena's final words to Sam echoed through her head: "Telling Deputy Cardwell won't solve anything." She fell asleep.

Uneasy dreams filled the night. Elena arriving at Sam's gala opening party, looking chic as ever in the turquoise that set off her blond hair so beautifully, draping the cashmere scarf over her chair, responding to someone's inquiry about how it was made. The scene shifted to the Tafoya home as Sam dropped Elena off, worried about how much wine her friend had consumed. Elena wrapping the warm scarf around her neck as she got out of Sam's car. The scene shifting rapidly, the scarf tightening around the slender throat, Elena's frantic attempts to scream for help. Sam stretching, reaching to save her, unable to quite do it.

She awoke in a tangle of sheets and blankets, panting.

"Wha—" Her breath came in gasps.

She sat up in bed and hugged her knees. The dream was clearly telling her that Elena needed her help. Her friend was reaching out and it was up to Sam to do something.

She switched on the lamp on her nightstand and picked up the phone. "Answer, answer," she pleaded, noticing for the first time that the readout on her clock said it was 1:47 in the morning.

Beau's mumbled hello was full of sleep.

"Elena Tafoya didn't kill herself," Sam blurted out. How could she convey the urgency of the dream?

"Sam?" He yawned hugely. "What's this about Elena? How would you know—?"

"Don't ask me *how* I know, please. Just trust me on this."

"Darlin, you do realize it's the middle of the night, don't you?"

"Sorry." She raked her fingers through her hair. "I just had this feeling that it couldn't wait. Do funeral directors work at night?"

"What?"

"You told me yesterday afternoon that Elena's body probably hadn't been cremated yet. But what if they work at night? What if they're doing it right now?"

She heard rustling in the background, the heavy comforter on his bed, perhaps. His hands running over a stubbly face.

"I don't know, Sam. They might be working tonight."

"Can you stop them? If they're about to cremate her? Please, Beau?"

"Let me make a call. I'll find out."

"Call me right back."

"Obviously, you're awake."

"I won't sleep until I hear from you." *I probably won't sleep anyway.*

"I'll let you know, no matter what's happening."

The dial tone hummed for nearly a full minute before Sam set the receiver down. She got up, wrapped her warmest robe around herself and found her sheepskin slippers. Pacing the floor seemed so cliché, but it was all she could do with sleep impossible and being completely at a loss for whom to call, other than Beau. She hovered within two strides of the phone until it rang. Eight minutes had passed as if they were eight hours.

"Okay," Beau said. "I had to call my office and find out which funeral home had her body. Turned out to be one in Albuquerque. I did reach someone there and I did get them to stop . . . working . . . on this until I get back to them. Now you want to tell me why the big panic?"

She took a deep breath and sat on the edge of her bed. If she were wrong about this, she was about to look like a huge fool.

"The scarf that Elena supposedly hung herself with—it was the same one she'd worn to the party at my shop, wasn't it?"

"Um . . . yeah, I believe so. It's in an evidence bag at the office. I could actually describe it to you if this call were taking place during my shift."

Oops, he sounded just a little ticked. "That's okay." She reminded him that he'd already told her it was the same scarf. "I just remembered something Elena told me about it, about how much she loved the scarf."

"She loved the scarf."

"Right. Don't you see? A woman wouldn't use one of her most prized possessions to kill herself."

"And why not? Maybe she wanted it to be the last thing that touched her skin."

Sam hadn't thought of that. "But—" In a dream Elena had called out to her . . . That wasn't going to fly, not in a murder investigation.

"How carefully did the medical investigator examine her body and the scarf?" she asked.

"Well, he would have examined the body pretty thoroughly. As far as I know, though, he didn't have the scarf. We bagged it and kept it here."

"But mainly, he just wanted to be sure she really died by strangling, right?"

"Yeah . . ."

"But I'm just not convinced. Elena was upset that night, yes, but I will never believe that she was so upset that she went right home and killed herself, Beau, especially not with her favorite scarf. I just—"

"Sam, with anyone else, I'd suggest that they get some counseling and work through the grieving process. Denial is always the first stage."

She started to sputter but he interrupted.

"But—listen for a second—you have good instincts. You've already proven that to me, and it's the only reason we're having this conversation." He paused for a moment. "I will get the wheels in motion for a revisit to the autopsy. I have to be specific in the request, based on some kind of evidence. I'll send the scarf to Albuquerque and ask the crime lab to do strength tests and . . . well, you don't need all the details."

She felt a tightening in her throat. "Thanks, Beau. Thanks for believing me."

"I'm also stepping up the pace on the Bram Fenton

investigation," he said. "And I can't promise that Elena's name won't suffer in the process. You have to be ready for that, hon. And you have to be ready, just in case it's proven that she did kill herself. Remorse is a powerful thing, Sam. It could be that she either felt guilty over the investigator's death or she might have panicked at the thought of being caught."

"I know." Sam felt the earlier burst of adrenaline drain out of her. Despite wanting to save her friend's reputation and memory, she might just be opening a whole new can of worms. She hung up the phone wondering if she shouldn't have left well-enough alone.

She switched out the light and crawled back under the covers but realized the futility of trying to sleep when she rolled over for the fourth time, only to stare at the red numerals on the clock that told her it was after three.

She pulled herself out of bed and moved quietly, dressing and leaving for her shop. She'd told Jen she would come in early but three o'clock was ridiculous. But, no matter. There was work to be done and lying in bed staring at the ceiling was pointless.

Yesterday's unseasonably mild weather had taken a complete turn sometime during the night. A frigid wind blew down Sam's lane, whipping tiny granules of sleet across her windshield. She tried to remember whether there was snow in the forecast. She pressed the button for the local station on the van's radio but they weren't on the air at this hour. No point, anyway. The weather would do whatever it would, no matter what some forecaster said about it.

By the time Jen and Becky arrived at six, Sam had finished

eight dozen orange-frosted pumpkin shaped cookies, a crumb cake, two cinnamon streusel coffee cakes and a batch of blueberry muffins. Becky took over with more muffins and some apple tarts, while Sam started creating the baby shower cake she'd sketched out yesterday. Soon she was lost in the decorating.

When Beau walked in the front door, Jen went into a fluster, as always happened when that six and a half feet of lean, hunky guy in uniform spoke to her. Sam couldn't believe it was already after ten; it seemed almost impossible that she'd awakened him after dreaming about Elena. Most of the coffee-and-croissant crowd had already come and gone.

"Maybe we should talk somewhere else?" Beau suggested.

For the first time in hours Sam looked out the front windows. The breeze still bent the bare tree limbs but the sleet had vanished. "A short walk might keep me alert," she said. She grabbed her jacket from its hook near the back door.

The thirty degree air nearly took her breath away after the warmth of the kitchen but she picked up her pace and kept up with Beau easily enough.

"So, is there any news?" she asked, almost the moment the shop door closed behind them.

"Actually, yes. I guess an early morning call, even from a county sheriff's deputy, carries some weight. The funeral home put the cremation on hold immediately. Then the MI's office got my message and collected the remains shortly after their office opened at eight."

It felt awful to hear Elena referred to as 'the remains' but Sam bit back a reply and tamped down her emotions.

"I don't know whether it's because of Carlos Tafoya's political prominence or if they just felt pushed to clear the case, but the medical investigator got right on it."

"And . . .?"

"And I sent one of our other deputies down to Albuquerque with the scarf. The guy wasn't especially happy to make the trip right at the end of his shift. But he left here about four a.m. and will probably be happy for the overtime."

"Beau! Get on with it. What did they find?"

"I quote: 'Upon closer examination of the ligature marks on the victim's neck, it appears that there are signs of strangulation aside from any marks made by the wool scarf.'"

Sam stopped in a crosswalk, ignoring the squeal of brakes from a car that almost didn't stop. Beau took her elbow and steered her toward the safety of the sidewalk before he spoke again.

"Yes, you heard that right. In the report they faxed to me, it seems that there were some bruising patterns. There was also a thin line, perhaps a cord of some kind. Overlying all that were the wider, softer marks made by the wool scarf. It was most likely grabbed up as an afterthought, a way to disguise the previous markings and to make it look like a suicide."

Sam stopped and looked up at him.

"So, you were right," Beau said. "She didn't choose her favorite scarf to, uh, do this."

Sam stifled her fleeting feeling of triumph. She didn't need to be right about this. She'd have given anything to have Elena back, alive and well.

"So, does this mean that the investigation will

continue?"

"You bet. Now that we know that someone else killed her, we have to pursue it as a murder."

They had reached the plaza now. The sidewalks were nearly deserted, in sharp contrast to the summer months when crowds of tourists packed the quaint shops and fought over parking spaces. Beau instinctively steered Sam toward the side that would keep them out of the harsh wind.

"Beau, I hate to think this but I have to say it. I think you'll have to look at our possible new governor as a suspect."

Chapter 19

His mouth formed a tight line. "How sure are you about . . . well, about the affair?"

"Elena told me. She wouldn't confess if she hadn't done anything." Sam pulled her coat tighter around herself. "I think Carlos found out. Maybe he grabbed her in a rage."

"There's just one big, giant hitch with that. Carlos Tafoya had an airtight alibi. Remember, he was giving a speech in Albuquerque. I'm pretty sure it ran late and he planned to stay over. I'll check it out, but when he's out campaigning he's got a whole slew of people around him. I will question them all but it's not likely that he could just leave without someone knowing it."

"Hm." Sam chewed at her lip. "Who else would have easy access to their house? Maids, gardeners, that sort of person?"

"Yeah, but what motive does a maid or gardener have to

kill the person who's writing their paychecks?"

She gave him a look that basically said *get real*. Employees always hate their bosses. But he was right. Nothing had been reported stolen. And the crime just didn't have the feel of an angry person who was lashing out. Another reason to discount either the husband or the lover.

"Maybe they had a houseguest?" she suggested halfheartedly.

"We'll be looking into it."

They'd circled the plaza now and Sam could see a half-dozen cars in front of her shop.

"I better get back," she said. "Hey, thanks for filling me in. I promise I'll sleep better tonight and I won't call you in the wee hours."

He pulled her close and stepped into a tiny alcove where two old buildings came together. The kiss was brief but nice.

Sam walked back into the warm, sugary air inside Sweet's Sweets, puzzling over the implications of the MI's findings and the increasing complicatedness of Elena's life. Sadly, she realized that she really didn't know much about her new friend despite the fact that they had hit it off so quickly. Elena's startling confession to an affair and a murder might well be just the tip of the iceberg.

Those thoughts continued to plague her as she handed out frosted cookies to the costumed kids who bombarded the store.

"Aren't they cute?" Jen whispered as a tiny ballerina left with her older brother, a ferocious vampire.

"No kidding—I remember being so excited over Halloween as a kid," Sam said. "Look at this next group."

She handed cookies to a space alien, a teddy bear, a

clown and a cowboy. As that bunch filed out a taller girl stepped in, replete with flowing black robes and a rubber witch face, including a green complexion and warts.

"Ooh, you look pretty scary," Sam teased.

The witch came in close, holding her hand out for the cookie. Her husky voice came out in a ragged whisper. *"The signs . . . will fall into place . . . Give them heed. The evil ones must pay but the seekers are in danger."*

"What—?" Sam leaped back and stared, her heart pounding as the witch accepted the cookie.

"Thank you," said the little witch in a completely normal child's voice.

Sam opened her mouth, but the witch had spun around and disappeared out on the sidewalk. Her hands shook as she noticed a fresh group of kids waiting for their treats. She handed out cookies absently. *Warnings from ten-year-olds?*

"Jen!" she called out the moment she had a break. "Did you notice that witch? The girl with the scary costume?"

"Sorry, no, Sam. I'd stepped into the back and the phone rang. We just got another order." She waved a printed form she'd carried from the kitchen. "Birthday cake for a ten year old, princess theme. I guess she's a princess until the price goes over thirty-five dollars."

Sam shook off the eerie feeling and took the form Jen handed her.

"One of the little princess's friends had the Cinderella cake, wide skirt with lots of flouncing . . . I guess ours wants the same thing. By five o'clock, if possible."

"Take over Halloween detail?" Sam gave Jen the cookie tray and walked into the kitchen, her mind still reeling. The warning voice had sounded uncannily like Bertha Martinez's.

She stared at the princess order, pulled the cone-shaped pan from the shelf, and told Becky to mix up chocolate batter and get it in the oven. She had pink and lavender buttercream already made for the baby carriage cake and she could easily use part of it to do Cinderella's ball gown at the same time.

"Becky, while you're at it, we better bake up some new fabulous thing for the Chocoholics group. If you have any brilliant ideas on that, I'll let you run with it. I'm a little stumped for them this week."

Focus, Sam. You can't take a kid's prank seriously.

"Sam? Earth to Sam . . . I was thinking—instead of cake," Becky said, "what about a triple chocolate cheesecake? Dark chocolate crust, creamy chocolate filling, mocha drizzle over the top . . . I saw something similar in a magazine and I think I could tweak it a bit, add some special touches . . ."

Sam forced her attention to focus. The Chocoholics. "Go for it. They'll love it."

Sam left Becky to that creation while she turned her attention to locating a doll form that would sit atop the elaborately draped skirt-cake. She made sure to include a few full-blown roses around the base of the cake as she put the finishing touches on it—what kid didn't love to pop a big old frosting rose into her mouth and swallow it down? And what mom didn't regret all that sugar, when bedtime found the little tykes still bouncing off the walls? The image brightened her mood considerably.

"What do you think, Sam?" Becky asked. "I practiced my roses earlier today. I think a big chocolate one in the middle of the cheesecake would kind of balance it nicely."

"Beautiful—you, kid, have a knack for this!"

Becky beamed at the praise.

"You can go ahead and deliver it to Ivan next door as soon as it's done. Their meeting isn't until tomorrow but I'm sure he would accept it today. Our fridge space is getting a little tight right now with the carriage, and I have to leave room for the Tafoya victory cake in there too."

The reminder of Elena caused Sam's smile to fade as she watched Becky working at the oven. She would have to ask Beau how the renewed investigation was coming along.

She got the chance to bring it up at dinner that night. She always loved driving out to Beau's small ranch on the north side of Taos. The open fields, green during the summer, were now fallow and dry, the view quickly dimming now at dusk. The two horses grazed in the distance; Sam had noticed that they normally stayed nearer the barn in the early mornings, awaiting the feed Beau scooped out for them. She still didn't make staying overnight at his house a regular routine, feeling a little strange about facing his mother clad only in one of Beau's shirts. And she definitely wasn't ready to call the relationship permanent enough to move some of her own clothes to his place.

This evening, he'd promised the stew that he'd made yesterday, along with cornbread and honey from a neighbor's hives. Anything she didn't have to bake, herself, was always appealing to Sam.

Ranger, the black Labrador retriever, and Nellie the border collie greeted Sam at the gates, trailing along behind her van as she negotiated the driveway up to Beau's impressive log house. He waved from the kitchen window and she walked in.

"Umm, smells good in here," she said.

He reached around her waist and pulled her close, savoring a long kiss. "Don't worry, Mama and Kelly are in the den, finishing a heated game of gin rummy," he whispered. She let herself enjoy the second kiss even more.

Voices from the living room distracted them. Sam took the basket of cornbread and Beau lifted the heavy tureen of stew.

At the dining table, Iris greeted Sam warmly and Kelly headed toward the kitchen to bring a green salad she'd made earlier. Sam noticed that Iris ate only a few bites of the hearty beef stew and her earlier vitality seemed to fade as full darkness set in. The elderly woman held out for a slice of apple pie but began yawning as the dishes were cleared.

"I'll get her set for the night," Kelly offered.

"Any news on the investigation?" Sam asked Beau, once they were alone in the kitchen again, loading the dishwasher.

"I *finally* got the judge to issue the search warrant I need on the Tafoya home," he said. "I'll tell you, maybe it's just my last name being so damned Anglo but it's not easy to get around the politics in this county."

"In this entire state."

"True." He handed her another dessert plate and she bent to put it in the dishwasher rack. "Anyway, after some real teeth-pulling I got the warrant signed. In the morning I think I'll have enough officers to properly execute the thing. I need at least two besides myself, three would be better."

"Can I help somehow?" she asked.

"That probably wouldn't be a good idea. The house is a crime scene now. We have to be careful with everything. I don't know why I'm saying that. Tafoya has had time to remove anything he wanted to, after all."

"Yeah, but would he? As far as he knows, everyone has bought into the story that Elena's death was a suicide, right?"

"That's all I can hope. We'll get an early start—hope to catch him in that pre-dawn defenses-down time of the day. I heard that he was in Roswell today—speeches and all that. And we know he was busy with the memorial service yesterday. With any luck, he'll be off guard."

"So he's definitely a suspect then?"

"No more than anyone else. I have to keep an open mind to everything I might find there. I just don't think it's really likely that he did it. Why would he risk his career right at this moment? He wants to be governor so bad he can taste it."

"Maybe he went into a rage. Struck out when he found out about the affair."

"But he was in Albuquerque that night. To sneak away and drive home and back is *very* premeditated."

Sam chewed her lower lip.

"His wife's affair would be a whole lot smaller scandal than her murder, wouldn't it?"

"And I guess her suicide almost works in his favor, right? Man hit by tragedy, the sympathy factor and all that?"

"Probably. Who knows what goes through the minds of the voters this week?"

Sam shook her head. She'd always wondered what went through the minds of the voters in this state—governors with horrible reputations for corruption, state legislators who had multiple drunk driving offenses, towns with local embezzlers and outright cheats—and they all managed to get reelected over and over again.

"We'll be looking for clues about Elena's state of mind.

Who she might have been in contact with during her last days, anyone who might have threatened her, someone angry enough that they would have killed her." He looked at Sam. "She didn't say anything to you along those lines?"

"I've thought about that a lot," she said. "And I can't come up with anything specific. But I have to admit that I was so shocked by her confession to killing the man who'd followed her that I probably missed other things. My mind was racing all over the place, knowing that it was Fenton she was talking about. Remembering the book with the coded pages we'd found at his place, thinking about the tests you'd ordered on the blood-stained coat."

She shrugged. "I don't know. I *really* hope I didn't miss something important."

"Hey, it's fine. The conversation probably wouldn't be admissible in court anyway. I'm just looking for someplace to start. I still have to come up with evidence."

Kelly peeked into the kitchen. "Hey you guys. I'm going to head home now. Iris is in bed, reading a large-print Agatha Christie. What time do you want me to come in tomorrow, Beau?"

He glanced at his watch. "I'll have to leave before dawn but I don't see any reason for you to be here that early. Mama will sleep until eight or so. Just come at your regular time and make her breakfast like you usually do."

Kelly gave a little salute and left.

"I better get out of here, too," Sam said. "You need to make an early night of it."

He agreed reluctantly and saw her to the door. "I'd sure like more time with you. Maybe after the election my boss will actually put in some time in the office, and we can convince Kelly to stay a whole weekend so we get away somewhere."

"Sounds nice." Sam kissed him and then pulled her fleece jacket tightly together in front against the bitter breeze that came down from Taos Mountain. He watched as she got into her van and gave a little wave as she drove out.

Kelly sat in front of the TV with a reality show blasting away as the contestants traded foul-mouthed quips with each other. Sam made herself a cup of tea and sat at the kitchen table to total her day's receipts and write up a bank deposit slip. She intended to browse her recipe files for new ideas but after nearly nodding off for the third time she gave up and headed for bed.

Darkness enveloped Sam and a stiff breeze howled upward, coming off the river at the bottom of the Rio Grande Gorge, carrying a sickly smell. She looked down and saw that she was wearing a dark green trench coat. She struggled vainly to shrug it off but the garment felt sticky. Her hands came away coated in blood.

Chapter 20

Sam woke from the dream in a sweat, although her bedroom felt freezing cold when she flung off the covers. She padded to the hall and checked the thermostat. It seemed all right and a quick touch on the baseboard register told her the heater was running just fine. A full moon lit the living room and kitchen, revealing dark lumps of furniture in all the right places. Sam gave it a glance and returned to her bedroom. Now, the temperature seemed fine.

On her dresser small dots of light winked in the darkness. Blue, red, green. They sparkled a few times and gradually blinked out. Odd. She'd never noticed the stones on the old wood box glowing, except for the times when Sam herself had picked up the object and held it. Had some unearthly spirit been in the room with her?

Goose flesh prickled at her bare arms.

The moon dimmed, throwing the room into complete

darkness. A shiver coursed through her and she dashed for her bed. Silly, she told herself. A bad dream, a hot flash, a trick of the moonlight. It was cloudy outside. That accounted for the moon glowing brightly and then disappearing. There are no ghosts, no visiting spirits, no *brujas*. She repeated it twice more before she relaxed. Calm, perhaps, but not tranquil enough to fall asleep for a long time.

Sam stood behind the counter when the first of the customers came in the next morning.

"I don't know what you put in those cookies yesterday," said a young woman with a baby on her hip.

"What?"

"My five-year-old, Damon. I tell you, he was bouncing off the walls after school. All that Halloween candy. I didn't want him to have more sweets but he got his cookie here and had half of it eaten before I could jump on him."

Sam held her breath. Oh, shit, what kind of lawsuit was coming her way?

"He calmed right down. At dinner he ate all his veggies, went to bed without a fight . . . So could I get a dozen more of those cookies?"

Sam gave a nervous chuckle. "I really didn't do anything special with them."

"I don't care. Whatever it was, it worked a miracle." The woman pulled out her wallet and pointed to the display.

"I only have three left."

"That's fine—I'll take them!"

Sam bagged the cookies and told the woman they were complimentary. The lady smiled widely and turned toward the door.

"I'll definitely be back!" she said.

After the fourth parent who commented on remarkable changes in their kids behavior, Sam called a staff meeting. Becky and Jen looked at their boss with wide eyes.

"Did either of you put anything—"

"Sam, no!" Becky protested vehemently. "I have kids. I would *never*—"

Sam held up her hands. "I'm not accusing. I just can't figure it out."

"We used all our standard recipes," Becky said. "Flour, sugar, butter . . . there was not one unusual ingredient in those cookies."

"And the food coloring came from a bottle we've used before," Sam mused, remembering that she'd tinted the frosting herself.

"I'm baffled," Jen said. "But, hey, maybe it was something else. Maybe the kids just had a fun day at school."

Sam didn't believe for a second that a school Halloween party explained a streak of sudden good behavior, but she wasn't about to voice her real suspicions. The mystical happenings that had surrounded some of her caretaking jobs now seemed to be spilling over into the bakery.

She let the girls know she wasn't upset with them and sent them back to their work. The Halloween cookies were gone now and there was nothing she could do to change the facts. She would distract herself by trying a new recipe.

She had come up with a pumpkin cake recipe and she would use a cream cheese filling and a glossy chocolate ganache icing. Today, she wanted to see how her regular customers liked it. Meanwhile, the ovens were full of cupcakes and muffins and cheesecakes. She chafed at having to wait for oven space. She really needed to work on test projects at home, in the evenings. The repairman was supposed to come this afternoon and Sam hoped that this time he really would show up.

The entire time she was trying to concentrate on accurate measurements and proper pan size, her mind echoed the warning from yesterday. The mask of the child-witch kept intruding into her thoughts. *The seekers are in danger.* That might refer to herself, but it surely meant Beau.

He was out at Tafoya's house today with his warrant, searching for the clues that would tell him what happened. Now that the medical examiner had found evidence that Elena's scarf had not killed her, Beau was intent on finding out who and what did. Some other person and some other device committed that crime. Not suicide. Murder.

She finally got the pumpkin layers into the oven, then managed to botch the ganache. Too distracted, she set the baked layers in the fridge and vowed to get back to it later. She dialed Beau's cell number.

"Hey there," he said. "What's up?"

Oh, a pint-sized witch spooked me yesterday and now I'm worrying that you're in danger, so much so that I can't even blend up a decent frosting. "Just thought I'd check and see how the search was going."

"Interesting . . ."

"Someone else is listening?"

"Exactly."

"How about if I meet you later? I just . . . it sounds silly, I know, but I need to know that you're safe."

"So far, so good," he said cheerfully. "I should be back in my office in another hour or so. I'm hoping to get out of there by five. No guarantees, though."

"I know you can't really talk. I'll catch up with you at some point. Maybe you can give me a call when you're free?"

He mumbled a half response, obviously distracted by someone else who was talking to him. They barely said goodbye before the line went dead.

Not exactly what I wanted to hear from him, Sam thought. But at least he didn't seem to be in any immediate danger. *See there, you little witch. He's fine.*

She went back to the ganache, turning out a perfect batch on the second try. She gave the cream cheese filling another stir, then quickly filled and stacked the layers. The ganache spread over the top, shiny and sleek, giving the cake a sophisticated appearance.

"This needs to chill for at least an hour," she told Becky, "but then I want to get it out for sampling. Can you help me keep an eye on the time, not let the whole day get away from me?"

Her assistant looked up from the tray she was filling with yellow and red roses, pre-making them for Tafoya's victory cake. "Sure. No problem. Are you going out?"

The idea took hold. Maybe if she just *happened* to be out for lunch . . . Beau's office wasn't that far away . . . And maybe if she *happened* to see his vehicle there . . .

As it turned out, he was just getting out of his patrol SUV when Sam cruised by and he spotted her. She whipped into a parking space and joined him at the sidewalk.

"So? I'm dying of curiosity since you described the search as 'interesting.' Can you tell me about it?"

"I shouldn't."

"Okay. Does it involve the bloody trench coat that was found at one of my properties? Doesn't that make me involved, just a little?"

"What is this, twenty questions?" He grinned and flicked at her chin.

"I can make it a hundred questions if you'll let me."

"Uh-huh. Well . . . no."

"Beau! At least tell me whether you have a suspect. I already know what the MI said." She looked around, realized that they were standing right in front of the sheriff's office. People were coming and going, although most were scurrying along to get out of the chilly November wind. "Can I take you to lunch?"

He glanced at his watch. "I don't have much time. There's a lot of evidence to process."

Another car pulled in beside Beau's in the spots reserved for Sheriff's Department vehicles. Lisa, the technician who always helped gather evidence at crime scenes. She had the knowledge and basic equipment for performing a few limited tests locally, but more complicated tests such as DNA and tissue matching were always sent to the state crime lab in Santa Fe. She greeted Sam as she walked to the back of her large SUV and began to pull boxes and bags from the back. Beau walked over and spoke to her for a moment.

"Okay," he said, turning back to Sam. "Let's take a quick lunch break."

They headed for a place two blocks over, a spot known for its hearty soups, which seemed perfect for a day like this. On the way, Beau began to talk.

"I found a heavy nylon bootlace that I think might be the murder weapon," he said. "Came across a pair of boots at the bottom of a hall closet, one is missing the lace but the other one indicates that the laces are pretty new, in good condition, thick and strong. So, I ask myself where's the other one? If someone used it to strangle Elena, what did they do with it? Didn't take too long to find it in a garbage bag out at the curb. Funny how people don't think things through."

"And you're pretty sure it's the one?"

"Without getting too graphic about it, let's just say that there's evidence of that, yes."

Sam pictured blood or tissue, but she stopped her thoughts right there. "So, you're thinking Carlos Tafoya?"

"The boots were a man's size nine, which fits with the other shoes in the home that belong to him. But—" he held up an index finger. "We don't yet have any proof that someone else didn't pull that lace and use it. A defense attorney would point out that anyone entering that house could have access to boots in the front hall closet."

"And Carlos wasn't home that night so it probably was someone else."

"Only the evidence will say for sure. A killer could have easily left his own DNA on the cord. Even with gloves there might be some traces of fibers or something like that."

Sam puzzled over that as they walked.

"There were a lot of different fingerprints in the master bedroom and bath, places you would normally only associate with the owner of the house. We finally got the maid to agree to being printed, for elimination purposes. The woman is Tewa, from the Pueblo, and I guess she believed that somehow the ink pad was going to read her spirit or some such thing. Lisa soft-talked her and took the prints right there at the house. We can find Tafoya's from our databases because all public employees have prints on file."

"What about other items? I'm still trying to work out

how Fenton's coat got to Cheryl Adam's house on the south side of town."

"In one of Carlos's coat pockets, I did find Fenton's business card. It's the first real proof that the two men had contact, although it's a far cry from showing that Carlos actually hired Fenton to track Elena. I gathered up most of the bills and other paperwork from his desk, just to see what we come across." He held the door to the restaurant for Sam. "Oh, one other thing you might find interesting. Elena kept a journal."

They stepped into the crowded room and a hostess immediately greeted them. Sam fidgeted, wanting to question him about the journal. Their table in a back corner afforded some privacy and people at the adjacent tables were engrossed in their own conversations.

"Could I see her journal?" Sam asked, shrugging off her winter coat. "I might be able to spot a clue in it, something that stands out because of the conversation we had, that final night."

He chewed at his lip, debating. "Normally, I'd say no way. Letting a civilian handle evidence can get into some sticky issues."

"But you deputized me, remember? Way back when."

"I know." He stared at the menu without really seeing it. "We've already dusted it for prints. And I'm really short-handed this week. Would you promise not to bend, fold or mutilate—or jot notes in it? And wear gloves while you handle it."

She sent him a look to let him know she wasn't that stupid.

"It's in my cruiser, unless Lisa finished carrying all the stuff we collected inside. I'll get it for you after lunch."

She smiled at him. "I really hope I can help."

Their server stopped by again, order pad at the ready, and they both chose the homemade vegetable soup.

"So, do you think there's any chance you'll have answers before the election?" she asked, once the server walked away.

"Not really. Anything going to the state crime lab will probably take weeks. I can always hope that we can match some fingerprints from our local databases."

"Maybe somebody will just show up and confess."

"I'd give better chances to a snowball in hell, Sam. Those things don't happen except on television. Especially if it involves somebody like Tafoya—no way a guy like that isn't going to lawyer up immediately."

Sam caught a sharp glance from one of the women at the next table, late twenties, dark hair cut in a sleek page, an oversized handbag on her lap where she was rummaging for something. Suddenly, their conversation felt a little too public. She tapped Beau's boot under the table. They started talking about the weather, and the dark-haired woman and her companion left a few minutes later. Sam watched them go outside and get into a blue sedan parked at the curb.

Their bowls of soup arrived just then and Sam gave her attention to eating, still mulling over what Beau had told her. She couldn't believe a married woman—a smart married woman—would actually reveal anything in writing, but there was always the chance of some little clue that would lead the investigation somewhere in a new direction.

Once they stepped back out on the street, Sam brought up the subject that had brought her to Beau's office in the first place.

"I'm worried about you on this investigation, Beau." *Although I can't really admit that a whispered message from a Halloween kid is the reason why.*

He draped an arm around her shoulders and brought her close to him. "So far, I haven't gotten any real sense of danger, Sam. Heck, this is a whole lot tamer than patrolling back streets where the drug gangs hang out."

"I know. But be careful. Please."

They walked the two blocks back to his office, pulling their coats tight against the increasing wind. Gray clouds sat low over the face of the mountains and tiny grains of sleet spat down in gusts. Beau located Elena's journal and handed it to Sam, extracting another promise that it would remain safe and intact. At her car, he paused and kissed her lightly.

"If this little sleet turns to snow, I want you to go home early. No sense being out in it."

"You too. You've got a lot farther to drive than I do."

His expression told her that leaving early was a dream. "If I get home late I'll call ahead and just tell Kelly to stay in our guestroom. It wouldn't be good for her to be out on bad roads either."

"Not for a girl who's spent the last ten years in southern California. Thanks, Beau."

Sam started her van and pulled onto the street, giving Beau a quick wave as he headed into the county building. She was nearly a block away when she spotted the blue sedan with the young, dark haired woman who had been sitting near them in the restaurant.

Chapter 21

The blue sedan sat at the curb and the woman was sticking coins into a parking meter, struggling to keep her dark green wool coat from flying open and shrugging her oversized bag onto her shoulder at the same time. Her neatly cut page was whipping across her face, obscuring her vision and making the job twice as difficult. It didn't appear that she had seen Sam.

Curious coincidence, Sam thought. Same restaurant, same street as Beau's office. She shook off the sense of worry. Taos is a small town. A lot of people plan their errands to get several things done in the same part of town at once. Silly to give it a second thought. But she couldn't help remembering how the woman had appeared to be listening to their conversation at the table.

At Sweet's Sweets Jen assured Sam that all was well. They'd had a larger than normal rush on cupcakes and cookies right after lunch, people stocking up with bags of goodies to take home for a quiet evening in front of the fire. The cheesecakes were all gone, too, she noted, as were the apple tarts and most of the cinnamon crumb cake.

Luckily, Becky had noticed the shortages. Four cheesecakes had just come out of the oven—their signature amaretto, a chocolate to be topped with raspberries, a pumpkin spice, and of course a plain one. She told Sam she'd also just put a crumb cake in to bake.

"You're wonderful," Sam said, admiring her new assistant's meticulous work.

Becky blushed slightly. "I've mixed up the dough for tomorrow's cookies and put it in the refrigerator. And the dry ingredients for muffins and scones—they're mixed and stored in those tubs. All we have to do in the morning is add the liquids and bake them."

"Great idea. That will save quite a bit of time. Especially if the roads are snowy and I'm a little late getting here." Sam surveyed the kitchen and made up a supply list, which she faxed to her wholesaler. "Ladies, if it stays slow this afternoon, or if the weather gets bad, feel free to close a little early. I have to meet a repairman at home, but you can reach me there if you need to."

She didn't mention that while she waited she intended to read Elena's diary, which was burning a hole through her backpack at this moment. Fifteen minutes later, she'd pulled the small book from her pack and was putting the kettle on for tea. Snuggled into a corner of the sofa, she opened the leather-bound book.

Familiar writing covered the pages. Sam felt a catch in her throat as she remembered her friend's written instructions for the cake that was to celebrate her husband's election. A decision soon to be made by voters. Sam tuned out those thoughts and concentrated on the pages.

The first entry was dated earlier in the summer. The initial entry seemed to indicate that this was Elena's first attempt at keeping a journal.

I don't normally put personal things into writing. But this summer has become too . . . what shall I say . . . too emotional, too revealing, too strange to ignore. I feel like I must talk about it with someone and yet I cannot. I feel as if my head will burst with this new knowledge. If not my head, my heart will surely break.

After that first one, the entries were more traditional, dated, beginning the first week of July.

Despite knowing it's wrong, I'm still seeing him, the man I shall refer to in these pages by the initial D. The first few pages discussed the very things Elena had told Sam on what was to be her final night. She was seeing a man, believed herself to be in love with him. D? The name didn't fit anyone Sam could think of but she read on. In spite of the fact that both were married, they wanted to be together, to leave their unhappy marriages and start a new life together. Then came the part that frightened Elena.

Someone may have seen me. I'm so afraid that I may be caught out at night in the wrong neighborhood. That the person might reveal my affair to Carlos. Or worse, to the media. Carlos's life revolves around becoming governor. The next few months will be crucial. If only he would lose the election and give up. Then I could leave and start my own life. But he won't. He'll never give up.

Another entry, three weeks later: *I'm now sure someone is spying on me. I might try to get a small gun for protection. I could probably ask for bodyguards, like Carlos has, because I'm the wife of the candidate. But that would only complicate things further. I would have to give up seeing my real love, and that is also impossible. It's better that I be ready to defend myself.*

Apparently the idea of the gun hadn't worked out, since Elena ended up with only the small knife. Two weeks went by with mundane entries about everyday life. Almost as if the fears and intrigues of Elena's life had disappeared. But Sam knew better.

In the second week of August came the entry she expected. Elena's normally elegant script was jagged and off-kilter.

Horror!!! I had the most—absolutely most—awful experience. The stalker caught up with me. I swung. I ran. I don't know what to do now.

Couched in vague language that didn't admit to the murder, nevertheless Sam knew what Elena meant.

The next entry was calmer: *It's been taken care of. D assures me that the awful deed will be noted as an accident. I don't know how—I'm just thankful to put this behind me. We have agreed to take a break, to see each other less often until November. I don't know how I will survive this but I shall.*

Sam found a yellow pad and jotted notes to discuss with Beau. Apparently the lover had disposed of Fenton's body, which explained a lot. No one of Elena's size could have lifted a grown man over the railing at the gorge bridge and dumped him. But another man . . . it made sense. It also made sense that the lover would now want some distance between them, and if Elena hadn't seen him in a few weeks it could very well be the reason that she broke down and confided in Sam. But Sam's sense of tidiness ended abruptly when she read the next entry.

The gross unfairness of it!!!! I hate him!!! My loving husband

— he is lower than scum. I've always suspected his affairs but now I learn this new fact. There is a child—a little boy!!!! He told me so, himself. The BASTARD! As if to rub my face in it!! He wants me to ignore his indiscretions while I am so tortured about mine??

Sam found herself reading faster, needing to know Elena's state of mind as this revelation had surely rocked her world. A child by someone else. Elena's own heartbreak over not having any children of her own, and now learning that he'd fathered a son, secretly. She turned to the next entry.

I cannot keep still about this. We screamed at each other half the night. He swears he has not seen the other woman in years—he finally tells me that she died in a car accident more than two years ago. He says the child has no idea who his father is, that he is now being raised by an aunt. Isn't that convenient for him?? I want to scream, to scratch his eyes out! I should tell that reporter about it, the one who interviewed me last year about our happy home life. That would teach Carlos a lesson. What would the voters think of him then?

The rest of the pages were blank. Sam's heart thudded.

What better motive for Carlos Tafoya to kill his wife? She'd confronted him and threatened to ruin his career. A bombshell like this, practically on the eve of the election? Oh, Elena, what did you do?

Sam dialed Beau's cell phone and read him the last two pages. "Do you suppose she actually confronted him and threatened to expose his secret?"

"Certainly points us to a motive, doesn't it?"

"But he has a pretty good alibi, doesn't he? Giving a speech in Albuquerque the night she died, a few hundred people witnessed that, didn't they?"

"I'd be surprised if a guy like Tafoya actually did the deed himself, Sam. He's got connections and bodyguards and henchmen who would do that sort of thing for him."

"True. But, geez, Beau. That sure opens him up to a greater risk, doesn't it? People like that wouldn't be exactly trustworthy in keeping a guy's secrets."

"You'd be surprised. If the money's right, a man can buy just about any kind of loyalty."

Sam grumbled but let it go. He was right.

"Have you looked outside recently?" he asked, changing the subject. "There's already an inch or more on the ground."

Sam peered around the edge of the living room drape. Sure enough, the ground was white.

"It'll probably start sticking to the roads pretty soon," Beau said. "Unless you want Kelly home with you tonight I think I'll suggest that she stay with Mama. I could get called out to handle traffic problems or something."

That seemed like the best plan. They ended the call with a few suggestive ideas but Sam knew they both had more on their minds besides getting romantic.

She'd no sooner hung up the phone than there was a tap at her front door. Oven guy. With a quick comment about the encroaching weather, he bustled into the kitchen.

"Got the part for your oven right here," he said, applying a screwdriver to the control panel. "Should just take a minute."

It was longer than a minute, but not by much. Three hundred dollars later, he was on his way. Sam made the entry in her checkbook absentmindedly, thoughts still bouncing around in her head, puzzling over what had really happened to Elena Tafoya.

At eight o'clock she peered out the window and noticed that it was, indeed, a white world out there. She went to bed wondering how much snow might possibly accumulate overnight, remembering that she'd not been out to check the Adams property in nearly a week and making a mental note to do that. She had two other properties under her care right now, but she'd thoroughly winterized them when the first of the cold weather came along.

By four a.m. she'd come to the conclusion that sleep was not coming back. A glance out the window showed that about four inches had fallen. The silent sky was black with pinpoint dots of light. In the distance she heard the grind of a snowplow, blocks away, probably clearing the intersections and major roads. If she left soon and took the back streets she could get to the shop before anyone else was out. The fresh snow and her four-wheel-drive pickup truck should make for easy traveling. Once the sun came out everything would clear by noon. She dressed quickly and reached into the wooden box for her watch and earrings.

Sweet's Sweets looked like something from a Kincaid painting with its softly glowing nightlights, snow sprinkling the awning like powdered sugar. Along the roadway and parking area the trees and shrubs stood as frosty sentinels with white icing mounded upon their branches. She cruised past them, circled the building and cut a path through the alley with the truck's wide tires.

Inside, she preheated the ovens and adjusted the salesroom's thermostat so it would feel cozy for the early customers. Becky's planning paid off—Sam added eggs and milk to the dry ingredients for muffins, divided batches and added spices and fruit, and soon had four dozen little golden pastries ready for the front room. Scones followed. Napoleons, chocolate cream puffs, apple strudel, and fruit tarts. She stayed in her own zone and relished the enjoyment of pure creation.

By the time Jen arrived at six, the place was filled with the scents of sugar, fruits and spices.

"Looks like all I have to do is add the coffee," she said. "Too bad we don't have a giant vent fan to send this heavenly smell all over town. We'd have customers lined up out the door."

As it turned out, they nearly did. It seemed that everyone who worked in the center of town and the plaza area had the same thoughts: warm, comfort food for breakfast on a day like this. The coffee, chai, hot chocolate and cider went out by the gallons. Office staff came in with orders and left with boxes neatly tied in purple ribbon and stuffed with dozens of assorted pastries. Riki walked over from her grooming shop.

"Hi luv, the scent of this place is driving me crazy over there, you know."

She browsed the cases and chose a blueberry tart and a hearty square of Becky's Pennsylvania Dutch crumb cake. Sam poured her a large latte and said, "On the house. Just send your customers our way, while they wait for their dogs."

"I'm already doing that, Sam. In case you hadn't noticed, you are the favorite spot on the block now."

Sam gave the slender British transplant a quick hug before she departed. She stayed in the front long enough to rearrange the displays and neaten things up before heading to the kitchen again to see how Becky was doing.

"Got it under control here, I think," Becky told her. "I'll have more muffins ready in a jiff."

"Okay. That's great. If you can handle things here, I need to get out to one of my properties and check it over."

As she'd assumed, in the midmorning sunlight the streets had quickly cleared, with brownish runoff in the gutters the only sign of the nighttime winter wonderland. The final spots of white were on the shady sides of buildings and shrubs. Sam climbed into her truck and headed south on Paseo del Pueblo Sur.

When she reached the turnoff to the narrow lane where Cheryl Adams's house stood, she remembered the downside of life on the edges of town. Hickory Lane showed deep, muddy ruts that threatened to be slick. She shifted the truck into four-wheel mode and steered carefully. At the Adams house a set of tracks veered into the driveway behind the coyote fence. Sam tensed. Someone had already been here.

But there was no vehicle in sight. Maybe they'd just chosen this spot to turn around. Pulled in and backed out again. She aimed her truck at the center of the small parking area and firmly established dominance of the space.

No footprints crossed the snow on this shady side of the house, no sign of disturbance in the frozen crystals that remained on the small porch. Sam crunched across them and unlocked the door.

Inside, the house felt cold, empty, and stale. She walked through to the kitchen at the back, surveying the living and dining rooms, checking the sign-in sheet that she'd left on the kitchen counter. No one else had logged in. Sometimes her contracting officer, Delbert Crow, checked the houses where she'd worked. Occasionally a Realtor showed a place. But no one had been here.

She went to the utility room where she verified that she had drained and turned off the hot water heater. The home's heating system was electric baseboard heat and each thermostat Sam checked showed that those were turned off.

She remembered shutting off the main water valve, and now she poured a little antifreeze into each drain as she walked through, a little extra insurance against the pipes freezing as temperatures began dipping toward zero in December and January.

A peek into each of the bedrooms. Checking latches on windows as she went, she came first to the smaller room, the one which had housed the Adams children. All was neat and clean here. Then she heard a sound.

She froze.

There it was again, the faint scrape of something metallic. She edged toward the master bedroom door, realizing the only weapon at her disposal was the plastic jug of antifreeze that she'd used in the kitchen and bathroom. A gallon jug, roughly half full of liquid—well, it might effectively clobber an intruder in the head. She gripped it tighter and nudged the bedroom door with her left hand.

Mini blinds at the windows cast thin stripes of sunlight across the brown carpet. The squeak sounded again, tiny, as if a wire hanger were slid along a metal rod. Her eyes darted to the closet.

A man stood at the open bi-fold doors, reaching into the closet as if he were hanging up a garment.

"Sir? What are you doing?"

The figure ignored her, just continued his perusal of the closet.

"Sir, you can't be in here. This house is under the care of the USDA."

He slowly began to turn. Then he simply vanished.

Chapter 22

Sam's heart stopped.

"What the hell—" She held up the plastic jug, a last-defense battering ram. But there was simply nothing there.

Her gaze sped around the room. Nothing.

She looked behind her, wondering if he could have possibly gotten past her. But how could that be? She'd never left the doorway.

She set the jug on the floor and edged her way into the bedroom. The closet was completely empty. What had made the metallic sound, what she'd taken to be a hanger on the rail? She rubbed at her eyes with her fists, realizing how cartoonish that move would seem to anyone observing.

Taking several deep breaths, she worked to steady her heart. *I know what I saw. A man. Standing right there. Putting something in the closet—or looking for something. He looked absolutely real. About my height, sort of round in the middle, dark clothing, a cap* . . . She struggled to recapture the vision but it was fading quickly, just as the man himself had vanished.

She strode to the window and pulled the cord to raise the mini-blinds. Dust motes drifted through the air as the room flooded with light. A perfectly ordinary room. An empty room. She lowered the shade.

Sam edged toward the door, keeping her eyes on the open closet doors, switching to stare out into the hallway as she neared it. Nothing. Not a shadow, not a sound, not a breath. She rushed down the short hall and out the front door, locking it and stashing the key in the lockbox.

Inside her truck, she locked the doors and blew out her pent-up breath. *Okay, Sam, think this through.*

There'd been one other time when she saw something strange—another time after she'd handled the magical wooden box—a greenish plant residue that provided an important clue in one of Beau's cases. And now she'd spotted this strange man near the place where the bloodied trench coat had once hung. *So, that's what I'll do*, she thought. *I'll tell Beau about this and see if it has any bearing.*

The truck started with a roar, the wheels losing traction as Sam gunned it too hard on the muddy road. She slowed, deciding it would be stupid to slide off the road because of a vision that she couldn't even really explain.

As she drove slowly through town she began to question herself. What had she actually *seen*; how would she explain it to Beau? At the street where she would normally turn to go to her shop, she almost did. Almost convinced herself that simply going back to work, ignoring ephemeral visions, creating visions instead in sugar—that would be far better than bringing this up to anyone else.

But then she looked down at the seat beside her, at the

plastic bag holding Elena's journal. Her friend's words came back to her, the desperation in Elena's voice when she'd told Sam how she'd slashed out at the man following her. How panicky she'd felt when the knife connected with his skin, when he began to bleed all over his coat. And then Elena's final words, words of hatred for the husband who'd betrayed her with another woman, the husband who had likely hired that man to stalk his wife. If Sam could offer any assistance at all, any small clue that could help Beau find the answers, then she owed it to him and to Elena's memory to offer it.

She drove past the square and turned left on Civic Plaza Drive. Beau's cruiser sat near the entrance, as if he'd been the first to arrive this morning and had managed to snag the best parking slot. Sam didn't get quite that lucky; the closest spot was more than a block away.

Crunching through little patches of ice in the shady spots, she hugged the plastic-clad journal to her chest and entered the sheriff's department. The clerk at the front desk recognized her and nodded toward the long hall that led to the offices and small lab.

"He's in Sheriff Padilla's office," the dark haired Hispanic girl said.

Sam took that as permission to go searching for Beau so she followed the hall toward the back of the building. Beau's own desk sat in an open room where several deputies normally took care of paperwork and did whatever computer research necessary for their current cases. The room was unoccupied at the moment.

Voices came from an open doorway on her right.

". . . for the record," said Beau's voice.

Sam moved closer

"For the record, *Deputy* Cardwell, I want no record of this."

"Sheriff—"

Sam paused outside the door, blatantly eavesdropping but ready to dash to the safety of one of the visitor's chairs if either man made a move.

"It's nothing, Deputy. I've visited the Tafoya home on several occasions. My prints could have been there for months. You know those Indian maids don't clean thoroughly."

Beau shuffled uncomfortably. "In the bedroom? It doesn't look right. If you're refusing to make this part of the record, Sheriff, it has to be reported to I.A."

"I'm not worried about Internal Affairs," Padilla said. "I've been in this town and in this department a lot longer than you."

Was he threatening Beau's job because of incriminating evidence against himself? Sam held her breath.

"Listen to me, Cardwell. I have an excellent track record as sheriff of this county. I clear my cases quickly and cleanly. And I'm not answering to you!"

"You have to answer to the voters of the county," Beau responded. "And I think they'd rather know their sheriff is an upright man, somebody they can trust."

Padilla seethed. "They do trust me. You're going to find that out when they go to the polls. This meeting is done."

Beau came stomping out the door and jolted to a halt when he saw Sam. He didn't speak but motioned with his head for her to follow him. She trotted along behind as he strode through the squad room and out a back door to the parking lot.

"What are you doing here?" he asked, his color high.

She held out the bag containing Elena's journal. "I brought this back."

"Sorry, didn't mean to bite your head off." He puffed out his cheeks and exhaled sharply. "Did you hear much in there?"

"Some of it. I gathered that you found the sheriff's fingerprints in the Tafoya's bedroom. He didn't have any explanation for that?"

"Said he'd been there once for a party and probably walked through the master bedroom in search of a bathroom."

"Once. As in, a long time ago? Would fingerprints be there after a long time?"

"Depends. On certain surfaces, under the right temperature and humidity conditions . . . yeah, we can sometimes get latent prints. Might expect them on a light switch, doorknob, bathroom fixtures . . . okay, that might fit the sheriff's story. What I didn't tell him is that these came from the cover of that journal you're holding. Which we found taped to the underside of a nightstand drawer on Elena's side of the bed."

"So he's held this book."

"Maybe in the bedroom, maybe somewhere else. I didn't tell him everything; I was hoping he'd come up with a logical explanation. But you heard how he was."

"Kind of it's-you-or-me, this town ain't big enough for the two of us."

"Yeah."

Maybe this was what the warning had been about. Sam thought about it, but she didn't say it. She changed the subject.

"Did you read any of the entries in this?" she said, holding up the journal.

He shook his head. "Lisa found it, printed it and bagged it."

"The final entry is dated the day before she died. In it, she's thinking of going to the press with Carlos's threats, revealing that he was having her followed *and* that he'd had a child by another woman. Elena rants about the unfairness of his double standard and it looks like she seriously considered wrecking his career because of it."

"Whoa." Beau stared at her.

"Motive enough?"

"It sure helps to establish it. I'll push the state crime lab to get any evidence they can off that boot lace." He glanced toward the building. "Quietly though. I can't risk Padilla pulling me off the case. For now, I think I better just keep my mouth shut and work around him."

"Be careful. Please?"

He gave her a light kiss. "I will. You know that, darlin'. I'd better get back inside."

Sam watched him go in, and it wasn't until she was in her truck, halfway back to Sweet's Sweets, that she remembered she'd hadn't told him about the ghostly image she'd seen in Cheryl Adams's house.

She debated whether to call him right back or to wait until this evening and talk to him at home. The latter won out, as she figured he was already in enough hot water with Padilla that he didn't need her adding more fuel to his boss's fire. Instead, she stopped in at the bakery and was pleased to see that everything was going smoothly there. Her final job for the day was to finish Tafoya's victory cake. The big party was to be held tomorrow night in the ballroom of the Arroyo Grande Lodge and as long as she had the cake there by five p.m. her duties would be done.

Becky helped her bring the large tiered cake out of the fridge and Sam set to work piping borders, creating a New Mexico zia symbol of gel and then surrounding it with the red and yellow roses Becky had made yesterday. She finished it with Elena's chosen wording "Tafoya, THE Answer for New Mexico," glad that she didn't have to write Congratulations.

Elena. How could anyone have known that the woman who ordered this cake such a short time ago would never live to eat a slice of it, to be at the very party at which the beautiful cake would serve as centerpiece? Sam worked with the frosting carefully, giving the confection her special touch, in memory of her friend.

"That's amazing," Jen said, standing back to look at the cake as Sam put her tools away.

"Very New Mexican, isn't it?" Sam said.

"Just what the customer wanted."

"I hope so." Sam considered the finished cake. "I really hope she would have liked it."

Jen put an arm around Sam's shoulder. "She would have loved it."

Beau called as Sam was pulling into her driveway at home.

"Hey there," she said. "I was thinking of calling you tonight. What's up?"

"Just saying hi. And, uh, wanting to apologize for being kinda short earlier in the day."

"What—a guy can't be grumpy when his boss is crawling up his rear?"

"Well, you know."

"It's fine, Beau. Really." She unclipped her seat belt and

gathered her pack. "Did you get a chance to look over those journal entries that I mentioned?"

"Yeah, briefly. I'd have to agree with you. Carlos Tafoya's political career could have been toast if Elena had followed through on her threat."

"So, does that give you enough evidence to question him?"

"Probably. But there's no way Padilla is going to let me do that right now. Election's tomorrow. If Tafoya loses, it'll be no problem. I'm sure we can bring him in and there would hardly be a flicker of interest. If he wins, that's going to be a whole other story. The new governor . . . a murder investigation . . . hell, at this point Padilla isn't even letting us release the news that Elena was murdered. He's letting the press and the rest of the world believe the original suicide story."

Sam set her pack on the kitchen table and shrugged out of her jacket, maneuvering the cell phone from one ear to the other.

"Beau, there's something else I forgot to tell you earlier." While she filled the tea kettle, one handed, she told him about the phantom man she'd seen in the Adams house that morning. Bless him, he didn't laugh.

"You said he was standing in front of the closet in the master bedroom?"

"I heard the scrape of hangers against the rod. That's what made me look into the room in the first place."

She could hear him take a deep breath and imagined that he was wrestling his unfailing common sense against the fact that he knew from the past that she sometimes saw things other people couldn't see.

"And he just vanished, right before your eyes?"

"I didn't believe it either. I rechecked the whole house."

"Did you recognize him?"

"No. I only saw him from the back. He was about my height, kind of pudgy, wearing dark clothing and some kind of cap. Just when he started to turn toward me is when he disappeared."

Again, a long pause. "I'm not quite sure what to do with this information, Sam. I can't very well put a bunch of people in a lineup based on this, can I?"

She laughed. "I guess not."

"At least you still have your sense of humor about it."

"At least you're not calling me a nutcase or sending the psych ward folks after me. Are you?"

This time he laughed. Turning serious again, he said, "I just wish we had some idea how the evidence—the bootlace, the journal, the bloody coat—ties together."

"And how to build the case against Carlos Tafoya."

"As much as I think that's how it's going to go, remember, Sam, we can't pick our suspect and then make the evidence fit."

"But who else could it be?"

"Elena admitted to you that she'd had an affair. What about the lover? A jealous rage because she wouldn't leave Carlos? We still don't know who this mysterious D is. We just don't have a lot to go on."

Sam pondered that after Beau hung up. Clearly, no matter how closely he might be tied to Elena's or the private investigator's deaths, making a strong case against the leading candidate for governor wasn't going to be easy.

Chapter 23

Kelly brought dinner home that night, leftover stew from Beau's house. "They'd eaten it three nights in a row over there," she explained. "Iris practically begged me to take the rest of it away."

Sam checked her email and found two new bakery orders from the website that Kelly had designed for Sweet's Sweets. She sent them to the printer queue and the little machine was chugging away when her phone rang again.

"Sam, please take me seriously on this," Beau said. His earlier playful tone was completely gone. "I know I should not be giving you inside information, but someone has to know and impartial people in this department are scarcer than hen's teeth, as I discovered when I tossed Tafoya's name into the suspect pool today. Looks like everyone in the this office is planning to vote for the man."

"Beau, what's going on? What aren't you supposed to tell me?"

"I got a call from the technician I've been talking to at the state crime lab, the one who said he would expedite the DNA test on the bootlace. The markers are very close to Carlos Tafoya's."

"So that's the evidence you need! That's a good thing."

"They're close. But not an exact match. It's someone related to him."

"And you don't want to make a huge issue of this because of the timing?"

"Well, yeah. Plus, I think the evidence is right. It's not Carlos. I'll probably have to start looking at his extended family. It's male, so a brother or his father . . ."

Sam flashed on an image of Victor Tafoya, her landlord. The crusty old man was known for being fairly ruthless in business, but he had to be in his seventies. She couldn't picture him strangling Elena and then managing to hang her body to look like a suicide. Maybe he helped, though. Handled the bootlace or something.

"Beau, that's not all though, is it?"

"No, it's not. I got a threat."

"What! Personally? Who's threatening you?"

"I don't know. An anonymous call."

"Because of the call from the crime lab?"

"Probably. I *told* the guy to call me on my cell, not the office line. But he forgot. Called the office first. He admitted that he'd left a message for me there before he reached me on my cell."

"Oh boy."

"Yeah."

"What did the anonymous caller say?"

"Just that I better back off and stay out of this."

"Isn't that essentially what Sheriff Padilla said earlier today?"

"Yeah, but not exactly in the same words. And it definitely wasn't his voice."

"Beau, remember how I told you to be careful? Well, that wasn't just idle conversation. I had a warning." She didn't mention the source. "It was a warning to 'the seekers'. In this case, I think that might mean anyone who is trying to solve this crime."

"Maybe the warning was meant for you, Sam." He paused. "Damn it, I shouldn't be involving you in this thing at all."

"Don't think that way, Beau. You're the visible one on the case. And now you've gotten this threat."

He assured her that he would take extra precautions, but she hung up uneasily. It felt like something bad was about to happen but she had no idea what. And she didn't have the benefit of a fresh dream from the old *bruja* to give new insight at the moment.

No portent came to her during the night, only a series of anxious dream vignettes, punctuated by twisted blankets and thrashing limbs. She woke at dawn with a headache and no answers. The wooden box glowed softly when she picked it up, easing her headache and warming her hands.

Her spice-scented shop was quiet in the light of the Taos sunrise, a little oasis of peace before Sam began the day. She brewed a pot of her signature coffee and helped herself to one of the first cranberry scones to come out of the oven. She relaxed and realized that her headache was completely gone. Worrying was not going to help Beau and it certainly wouldn't solve his case for him. Everything in its own time, she reminded herself.

Jen arrived at six. "Whew, traffic is already picking up. Election day and the early risers are out." She set right to work making more coffee and readying the display cases with the new day's wares, and before she'd unlocked the front door people were pulling up in front of the shop.

"Let's make the most of it," Sam said. "Go ahead and open early."

Becky had taken the day off; with her kids out of school she needed to be at home. But Sam had the kitchen under control with fresh, hot pastries coming out every half hour or so. When a short lull came just before noon, she called Jen away from the counter to help load the victory cake into the back of her van. Sam called ahead to the hotel to be sure she could deliver it early and promised to get back to help Jen with the lunch and early afternoon crowds.

Jen was right about the traffic, Sam decided as she negotiated her way along the narrow streets near the plaza. Her destination was off Kit Carson Road, down a skinny lane that seemed an unlikely place for one of the town's more upscale hotels. Luckily, the weather had warmed and all traces of yesterday's snow were gone. She wouldn't have wanted to drive this route if it were icy. The roadway became wider, opening to reveal a tall, stately adobe building with an arched portico at the front, surrounded by ancient cottonwoods that still held a few of their golden leaves. The ground had already been raked clear of the thousands that must have fallen with the storm, revealing neat planters of brilliant chrysanthemums and dark evergreens.

She bypassed the sweeping entry and found a service

entrance at the back, parked the van and went inside to find out where the cake would be set up.

The ballroom teemed with activity. Hotel staff had already set up tables and chairs for the guests, a podium for Tafoya's expected victory speech, and long buffet tables that would later accommodate a hefty spread. Campaign volunteers were busily hanging huge posters that sported the now-familiar slogans and Carlos's smiling face. A compressor hissed air into red and yellow balloons which were then gathered into massive nets. Two of the filled nets already hung from the twenty foot ceiling.

Sam spotted Martin Delgado, the Tafoya campaign manager, and Kevin Calendar, the young campaign worker who seemed to be everywhere Carlos Tafoya went these days. Both of them would probably land plum jobs in Santa Fe when this was all over.

A woman with a clipboard noticed Sam's bewildered expression and approached.

"I need to know where the cake will be placed," Sam said after introducing herself and handing the woman her card. "Preferably where it won't be disturbed once I've set it up, and out of harm's way." She glanced at the balloons and nets and ladders a little uneasily.

The woman led her to the back of the room, where the decorating seemed to be finished. "Coffee and dessert will be served from this table. It should be safe here."

"And I need a hand, just for a minute, to lift the cake from my van."

"Sure." The woman scanned the room and raised an index finger. "Kevin! Need you here for a moment."

He spun at the sound of his name, sending her a look that Sam couldn't quite read. Dressed in dark slacks, white shirt and tie, maybe he thought he was above doing the heavy lifting. Sorry, kid, she thought. You can't be more than twenty, so you don't have a whole lot of seniority here. Too bad for you.

Kevin walked with Sam back through the kitchen and out the delivery door as she briefed him quickly on what they needed to do. He followed her directions as they placed the large cake on a rolling cart from the hotel kitchen. Negotiating their way through the maze of kitchen equipment proved a little tricky but they soon had it in place on its draped table at the back of the ballroom. Kevin wandered off, on to more important-looking tasks. Sam surveyed the cake placement, deemed it good, and set off to find the clipboard lady so she could get a signature.

A stir rippled through the room, grabbing her attention.

Carlos Tafoya swept in, looking very gubernatorial in a designer suit. The young workers tended to blush and lower their gazes as he passed. The clipboard woman approached him with a brief question which he seemed to answer with one word. She slinked off and Kevin Calendar approached the candidate in her place. Tafoya bent and whispered something to the young man, who tensed visibly. With hands clenched he stomped off to the opposite side of the room, glaring at the oblivious woman with the clipboard.

All at once, a wave of energy roared toward Sam like a riptide. She swayed backward at the force of it. *What the–?*

She straightened and took quick stock of the others in the room. No one else seemed to have noticed the nearly-visible energy field. Tafoya was still standing near the doorway, surveying the room, smiling at the sight. Clipboard-lady was speaking to two young women who were sticking posters to the walls with tape. Two reporters with shoulder bags full of recording gear were hanging close to Tafoya, apparently getting background to use for the evening newscasts. Something seemed familiar about one of them, but Sam didn't immediately make a connection. Before her brain could click, her attention wandered across the room again.

Kevin, the young campaign worker, had a reddish glow around him. *Oh, no. Not this again.* Sam watched as the redness deepened and became murky. The guy's face was nearly obscured by the intensity of it. *What on earth—?* As she watched, the glow faded slowly to nothing. She searched his face for a sign of strong emotion but nothing seemed out of the ordinary. He was merely watching Tafoya, but then so was everyone else in the room.

Sam shook off the feeling. She'd promised Jen that she'd get back to the shop right away and this errand had already taken longer than planned. She swung through the room, tapping the woman on the shoulder, getting her signature and handing over a copy to add to the stack of pages on her clipboard.

"Mrs. Tafoya paid for the cake in advance," she said. "This is for your records."

The woman gave her a harried smile, instantly distracted by someone else. As she walked past Carlos Tafoya, he reached out to shake her hand. "The cake looks very nice," he said. "I thank you for doing it, and for being Elena's friend."

Flattery always worked and Sam found herself automatically smiling back at him.

"I hope you can attend the party tonight," Tafoya said. He reached into the pocket of his jacket and pulled out a slip of heavy paper. "A VIP ticket. Bring someone if you'd like." He pressed it into her hand and bestowed another of the well-known political smiles. Then his attention was off to the next person who walked by.

Sam slipped past his little entourage, glad to be leaving the bustling room. She'd reached Kit Carson Road again before she remembered that she really ought to do her own civic duty by voting. The day probably wasn't going to get any less busy. She called the shop to check on Jen, who assured Sam she could handle it on her own for awhile longer. Sam drove the back streets to the high school, her neighborhood polling place.

As she stood in the voting booth awhile later she stared at the names on the ballot. Despite her fondness for Elena she would never trust Carlos. She marked her ballot for his opponent.

She was halfway to her van in the parking lot before she realized that the vehicle parked beside it was Beau's cruiser.

"Sorry, officer, I didn't mean to overstay my parking time," she said, approaching the window that he lowered as she walked toward him.

"Well, ma'am, I'm afraid I'm going to have to cite you anyway. The charge is being way too beautiful for a weekday and working far too hard for your own good." He grinned at her and reached out to run his index finger over her hand.

"Ha! Beautiful?" She glanced down at her black slacks and white baker's jacket. "This outfit hardly qualifies as glam."

"No, but the lady wearing it does."

"Why is it that I suspect you of being more than just a little horny?"

"Because you have some kind of psychic intuition and

you are exactly correct. Maybe tonight we should . . ." His radio squawked.

Sam drummed her fingers on the edge of the open window, wishing he'd had the chance to finish the thought.

A static-filled voice came at him and Beau answered with, "I'm there. Ten minutes." When he turned back to Sam it was with a rueful expression. "I'm wanted at the office."

"More hassle with the sheriff?"

"Not today. He's out glad-handing the blue-hairs at the senior center. Right now it appears that I have a visitor from Albuquerque."

"Really?"

"It's an intern from the crime lab. They ask each of them to ride along with law enforcement first responders as part of their training. Usually they get a city officer, somewhere like Albuquerque or Santa Fe, but then it's also good to observe a more rural setting. So, our department gets them now and then. When I talked with the lab yesterday they warned me the new kid was coming up here."

"Ah. Well, good luck with it."

"Which reminds me—remember that odd DNA match I told you about? The evidence on the bootlace showing that someone related to Carlos Tafoya handled it? And remember the entry in Elena's journal, saying that her husband had a child with a former lover?"

Sam nodded.

"The office rumor is that the kid is now grown. A grown son with the DNA markers that point to Carlos Tafoya as his father . . ."

Sam felt her eyes widen. "Carlos Tafoya's son might have been in their home? Might have—"

"You got it. It still seems farfetched to think he would go after Elena. It's not as if he knew her."

Sam's head swam, trying to piece together the bits of information floating around in there. "Can you just question him?"

"If we knew who it was, we most surely would."

"The diary didn't name the lover or her child, did it?"

He shook his head. "And I can't get my stubborn boss to let me question Tafoya."

Sam thought of the mammoth party being set up at the Arroyo Grande right now. A lot of people firmly believed that Tafoya would be the next governor of the state. "Time really isn't on your side here, is it? I mean, once Tafoya wins the election—if he does—he'll make himself so bulletproof that it'll be impossible to force him . . ."

"Exactly."

"Well, there have to be other ways to find the mother and the son, right?"

"Oh sure. It's just that it's pretty labor intensive to track down friends and neighbors who may have heard rumors, which may or may not check out, all from twenty years ago or more. We just don't have the manpower right now."

"Let me give it some thought," she offered. "Maybe something will come to me."

"I plan to review Elena's journal again. There might be a name or location that I overlooked before." He turned the key in the ignition. "Meanwhile, I guess I'm off to escort a rookie lab technician around."

Sam watched him drive away, feeling his frustration at being under budget and out of the loop with information his boss clearly didn't want uncovered. She pondered that idea as she got into her van and pulled away from the crowded parking lot. What if Orlando Padilla knew a whole lot more about this whole thing?

The idea took hold and when Sam spotted a Padilla For Sheriff mini-bus turning at the plaza, she followed. Sure enough, a little rally seemed to be forming up, with banners strung between the trees and people waving placards. They got excited as the bus rolled to a stop; the candidate must be aboard. Knowing she'd never get a parking spot anywhere near the busy plaza, she cruised past it and parked in front of her shop.

Sticking her head in the door she called out to Jen. "Can you spare me for a few more minutes?"

Her assistant looked startled. "Uh, sure. It's pretty quiet right now."

Sam speed-walked back to the site of the rally, which was now gathering momentum and becoming quite the noisy little fiesta. Standing on top of an impromptu platform that was actually a plywood box, Orlando Padilla in his felt Stetson was grinning hugely and waving at the crowd, announcing his thanks over a portable PA system of some kind.

Two reporters shouted questions and held microphones out toward the sheriff. Sam had to admit that the man could put on a show. His entire demeanor was different than when she'd met him on other occasions, times when he was actually performing his job instead of being dramatic for a crowd.

He handed off the microphone to a helper and stepped down from his little stage. Shaking hands and smiling, he worked the crowd until it began to disperse. Just before he could open the door to his bus, Sam stepped forward.

"Sheriff Padilla, could I have a moment?"

He turned with a smile, which went a little south when he recognized her. She forced herself to smile at him, not letting her true feelings show.

"Could we talk privately? Just for a minute."

He started to make an excuse but she'd placed her hand around his elbow making it awkward for him to brush her off. They walked a few steps, looking to anyone who might observe, like two old friends taking a stroll.

"Elena Tafoya was a friend of mine," she said.

Padilla stiffened, coming to a halt in mid-stride.

"I want her murder solved and I think you are deliberately leaving your deputies out of the loop."

His public smile had become a grimace. "Ms. Sweet, you're out of line."

"Am I? I think you have information that could help solve two murders that your department hasn't been able to close. You haven't talked much about them during your campaign, but this election day isn't over yet."

"Is that a threat? Because I assure you—"

"Threat, Sheriff? Of course not. It's a request for information."

His eyes narrowed. "What kind of information do you want?"

"Um, let's start with truthful information. Like the name of the woman Carlos Tafoya had the affair with. This would be some years back, but I believe you and he were very chummy, even back then. Somehow, I get the feeling that you helped him sneak around, provided him with alibis, that kind of thing . . ."

She could practically see the wheels in his head turning.

"Say that I did—what of it?"

"How would it affect you? Probably not at all. I just need the name of his lover, please. Where she lived, how to get in touch with her now."

His eyes narrowed, trying to figure out whether the conversation could backfire on him. Apparently he decided that he was safe; the information wouldn't get very far before the polls closed this evening.

"She lived in Tres Piedras twenty years ago, moved to Albuquerque after the relationship ended."

"And her name . . ."

"Jean. Jean Calendar."

It took Sam a few seconds to process the fact that it was the same last name as the young man she'd just spoken to at the Arroyo Grande Lodge. Kevin Calendar was Carlos Tafoya's son.

Chapter 24

Orlando Padilla had turned away and was walking across the shady square in the center of the plaza, headed back to his campaign bus, by the time Sam gathered her wits. She spun around, another question on her lips, but his retreat sent a spear of ice down her spine.

"Sheriff! Wait!"

He slowly turned, disdain on his face. "You said one question, Ms. Sweet. I believe I answered it."

"But—"

He'd already continued walking resolutely toward the waiting bus. Sam watched as a young man with ingratiating manners held the door for the sheriff. Padilla stepped up into the mini-bus and it started moving the minute he'd taken his seat. She saw his eyes following her as the bus drove out.

"Whatever you said to him certainly got his attention,"

said a voice behind Sam.

She started. When she turned, she saw a dark page haircut and billowing dark green wool coat. The young woman was standing at the curb, about twenty feet away, her hand on the handle of a blue sedan.

Sam stepped toward her. "I've seen you around. Who are you?"

The woman reached into a pocket of the coat and pulled out a business card. "Sandy Greene. Santa Fe *Times*."

Sam's eyes squinted as she stared at the card. "Why has a Santa Fe newspaper sent a reporter here to Taos?"

"Shouldn't that be pretty obvious? It's an election year. We cover all the races in the northern part of the state." She smiled prettily. "Well, I'm off to get a few more pictures." She patted the side of a camera case that hung from a shoulder strap.

Sandy Greene got into her car and Sam watched her drive away.

Itching to fill Beau in on her new findings, Sam dialed his cell as she walked slowly back to the bakery. She fumed when it went to voice mail but realized that his day was undoubtedly running on task overload. She left a message: "Gotta talk to you. Call me when you get a minute."

Sweet's Sweets was bustling with after-lunch customers wanting cake or pie to satisfy their need for sugar and boost them into their afternoon work world. Sam joined Jen behind the counter, boxing up chocolate nut drop cookies, macadamia nut wafers, amaretto cheesecake, and the new pumpkin spice cake with the ganache icing which they'd had trouble keeping in stock ever since they introduced it.

By five o'clock Sam felt dead on her feet and Jen remembered that she'd never eaten any lunch.

"You go," Sam told her. "Get something to eat and rest up. I'll get the kitchen in order and head out of here shortly, myself."

She locked the front door behind her assistant and turned on the night lights. Daylight was fading quickly by the time Sam walked out and got in her van. A voicemail symbol showed on the front of her cell, obviously something that had come in while she was buzzing around the bakery at such a pace that she'd never noticed it. Beau. She dialed him back.

"Hey," he said. "I just got my rookie back on the road to Albuquerque. Your message sounded kind of urgent. Everything okay?"

"Yeah, fine. I got so busy at the shop today that I almost forgot I'd called you." She filled him in on the fact that she'd learned the name of Carlos Tafoya's lover from all those years ago, and the name of his illegitimate son. "Kevin Calendar is working for the campaign. I've seen him around several times and I'm not sure why I never noticed the resemblance to his father."

"But then, why would you?" he said. "Why would anyone? I'm guessing the son never lived around here until recently."

"That's what I'm interested in knowing, too. When did he show up on the scene in Taos? And is his mother also here? Maybe Elena's fears were justified. Maybe part of the reason Carlos had begun to treat her so badly was because his old lover was back."

"It certainly bears asking him some more questions, I'd say. Not to mention that I'd like to get Kevin's DNA and see what he has to say about it showing up on the bootlace that killed Elena, assuming it's a match."

"Questioning Carlos is going to get nearly impossible, don't you think? I had the radio on in the kitchen awhile ago and the exit polls are making it sound like he's pretty sure to go to Santa Fe. Once he's sworn in as governor he'll find ways to make himself legally bulletproof, won't he?"

"Seems to be that way with these guys, doesn't it?"

"I have an idea how you could get to him right away. I happen to have a personal invitation from the candidate himself to attend his victory party tonight. He's at the Arroyo Grande Lodge."

"I'll pick you up in fifteen minutes," Beau said, clicking off the call before Sam had a chance to utter another word.

She drove like a bat, skidding the van to a stop in her driveway and dashing into the house, hitting her closet with a vengeance to find something to wear to a party. She settled on black slacks—a dressier pair than her normal work pants—and a sequined top. As she sat at her dresser, rummaging through her jewelry box for a fancier pair of earrings, she took a few seconds to let the wooden box send a nudge of additional energy her way. By the time Beau arrived, still in uniform, she'd run a brush through her hair and managed to slap on a little blusher.

"Hey, you sure look delectable," he said, giving her a smile that made her wish they were just staying in, alone and undisturbed by murders and such.

"Probably too much, huh. I just thought they might not let me in the door in a batter-stained baker's jacket."

"I like it." He pulled her close for a kiss. "Well, let's go interview a killer."

The Arroyo Grande Lodge's parking lot was filling quickly. The polls would be closed in another thirty minutes and the excitement was evident in people's posture as Sam watched them rushing toward the lobby entrance.

Beau, in his cruiser, ignored the whole protocol of parking and pulled up to the curb out front. While the crowd flowed down a central corridor toward the ballroom, Beau and Sam approached the front desk. He flashed his badge and said that he needed Carlos Tafoya's room number.

The young clerk, clearly briefed to never give out a guest's information, much less that of the future governor, looked bewildered at the sight of the badge.

"Please get your supervisor," Beau requested, with just the right amount of charm.

A little back and forth, and the manager passed a small slip of paper across the desk. They took the elevator, even though there were only three floors in the hotel. Beau tapped gently at the door of Suite A and it was opened almost immediately by none other than Kevin Calendar. The young man looked at Sam, trying to place her. Beau stepped forward, not giving him the opportunity to deny them entry.

The suite, probably the hotel's largest, featured a spacious living room decorated in traditional Mexican furniture and brightly patterned Indian rugs. A large flat-screen TV set was tuned to a news channel, where the anchors were making small talk until actual precincts could begin sending their results. Doors, presumably leading to bedrooms, stood closed on either side of the living area.

Carlos Tafoya sat on a leather sofa beside a thin woman with chin-length yellow hair. She stared at Beau's uniform, clearly concerned about why the law might be showing up. Tafoya jumped to his feet and started toward Beau.

"Is there anyone else in the suite?" Beau asked, his right hand hovering near his handgun.

"No!" said Carlos.

Beau peeked quickly into each of the bedrooms and then lowered his hand.

When Kevin circled to stand behind the sofa where the other two had been seated, Sam immediately noticed his resemblance to both parents. With his mother's fair coloring and his father's dark eyes and full lips, there was no denying the origin of his genetics.

"This is really cozy, but sort of bad form, don't you think?" said Sam. "Your wife died less than a week ago."

Jean Calendar flinched, her gaze flicking warily toward Carlos. Kevin glanced toward the door but Sam and Beau stood between him and the escape route.

"What do you want?" Carlos demanded.

"I need to ask your son a few questions," Beau said. "And I'll need a sample of his DNA." He pulled one of those little self-contained swab kits from his pocket.

Carlos looked over at Kevin. "He should have a lawyer." Sam noticed that Tafoya didn't bother to deny the statement about Kevin being his son.

"He's not a minor, so he gets to make that decision himself. You're not under arrest," Beau said to Kevin. "I can do this quickly, right here, or we can take it downtown." He met the politician's gaze with a level stare.

Kevin shifted from one foot to the other. "What's this about?" He tried to ask it with a show of bravado but everyone noticed that his voice was pretty shaky.

"We've found familial DNA markers on a piece of evidence. We're simply taking samples to eliminate non-suspects." The way he phrased it seemed to make Carlos relax a bit. He gave his son a nod and Kevin opened his mouth so Beau could swab it. He clipped the container shut and put it in his pocket.

"Would you rather answer my questions privately?" he asked Kevin, giving a nod toward one of the closed doors.

"He can speak in front of us," Carlos said. Jean had not uttered a sound so far, Sam noticed. Kevin nodded agreement.

Convenient, she thought, that Kevin wouldn't be able to say anything that his influential father wouldn't know about.

"Okay then," Beau said. "Shall we sit down?" He ushered Kevin toward the other end of the large room, to a dining table of heavy, carved pine. Pulling out one of the four chairs he didn't give the dark-suited young man much choice but to sit down. Carlos began pacing the floor, glancing now and then at the TV set which was muted now. Jean had begun to chew at her nails, Sam noticed as she parked herself in a side chair near a large armoire-bar setup.

"Now, Kevin, I need to ask you where you were a week ago Saturday, the night Elena Tafoya died."

Kevin stared at the grain on the wooden table. "Uh, I think I was out with friends."

"I'll need their names." Beau pulled out a small notebook and pen, poised to write.

"Uh, I really don't remember who all was there."

"Just a name or two?" Silence. "Okay, then, where did you go? A bar, restaurant?"

"A restaurant. I don't remember which one." As Sam watched, a dark blue haze formed around Kevin's face.

"You know for sure that you went out that night, but you don't remember anyone you were with or where you went?" Beau laid the notebook on the table and tapped his pen against it.

"No! I don't!" Kevin's voice rose in agitation. The blue haze became murky, then began to turn red. "I don't have to explain anything to you! And I don't give a shit what you think!"

His eyes were wild now, as he stared at the faces around the room.

His mother bit furiously at her thumbnail, tears forming in her eyes. She glanced up at Carlos—quick, nervous little pointed looks—but he didn't notice.

The politician's attention darted between the numbers rolling along at the bottom of the television screen and the situation with Kevin.

"I am not a bad person!" Kevin screamed. He jumped up, sending his chair flying.

Beau was on his feet, almost in a blur, facing down his suspect with a firm stance. But Kevin was quick, too. He bolted toward his father.

"You promised! You said we would be a family. You and me and Mom, and we were going to move to Santa Fe—together. But you had *her*! Nothing was going to work right as long as *she* was around."

"Kevin, I—" Carlos stepped forward, reaching toward his son.

Kevin shook him off, continuing his rant. "You told me you were filing for divorce. You said you had some kind of evidence on your wife and that she would let you go without a fight. But when I got there that night, she was *there*, all cozy and comfy in her robe. She wasn't moving out—she wasn't leaving you! You liar!"

"You went to their house that night?" Beau asked. His stance was alert as he watched Kevin shaking his fists at Carlos.

Spittle formed on his lips as he shouted. "I went to get some papers for the campaign. She wasn't even supposed to *be* there. She'd been at that bakery thing, that *party*. Then I thought she would go to somewhere . . . wherever she was supposed to be living because you were *divorcing* her. But she was *there*!" His skin had turned the same muddy red as the aura Sam had seen when his mood began to turn.

"Kevin, what did you do?" Beau's voice was icy calm.

The young man turned on him, staring with crazed eyes. "She said she would get the campaign papers, and then she went into the study. I saw some hiking boots near the front door . . ."

Sam saw the whole ugly picture unfolding. The bootlace around Elena's neck as she bent over a desk, her body being dragged into the bedroom, her lovely cashmere scarf around her neck and then draped over a heavy beam at the ceiling.

Kevin suddenly turned his attention on Sam. "How do you know that?" he hissed.

Had she spoken aloud? She glanced at Beau and saw that he seemed just as bewildered by the comment as she.

Movement caught her attention and she turned just in time to see Kevin lunge at her.

Chapter 25

In a flash, Beau leapt across the open space and threw an arm around Kevin's neck. Sam watched, amazed, as he did some kind of kick that took Kevin's legs out from under him. Pinned to the floor, Kevin flailed until Beau got handcuffs on him. Without a glance at anyone else in the room, Beau keyed his shoulder mike and called for backup.

Keeping a knee in the middle of Kevin's back, Beau looked up at Sam. "You okay?"

"Yeah." Her voice came out a little on the shaky side, but Kevin hadn't actually touched her.

Beau kept an eye on Carlos, watchful in case the older man should attempt to free his son, but the politician seemed to be more concerned with himself.

"I didn't know anything about any of this," he swore to Beau.

Jean was openly crying, sobbing into her hands, her

body a limp blubbering mass on the sofa.

Carlos turned to face his son. "I can't believe—" he stammered. "Kevin? Why would you— Elena?"

Beau recited Kevin his rights, finally eliciting agreement that the young man understood what he was being told, even as he continued to spew invectives at both Beau and Carlos.

Sam stood with her back to the wall, stunned at the show going on before her. Kevin's red aura was fading to a dull burnt orange now; Jean was surrounded by a white fog; Carlos's was a bright lemon yellow. She didn't know what any of it meant and was glad when a deputy arrived to take Kevin away. Jean followed quietly, hardly speaking to Carlos, murmuring something about being with her son.

Carlos continued to plead ignorance of the whole thing, even as he watched his son being hauled away in handcuffs and his former lover nearly becoming a zombie in her own confusion. He poured himself a half-glass of scotch at the bar and stood at the window, gazing down at the parking lot as he downed it in three gulps.

Beau pulled Sam aside. "I'll be tied up with the paperwork for awhile . . . He glanced at Carlos on the other side of the room.

"He's not going anywhere," Sam said. "This hotel, the victory party downstairs . . . it's exactly where he wants to be right now. I'll call down to the ballroom and get some more of his entourage to come up. We'll keep an eye on him."

"I wonder how many other people know anything at all about what happened," he said as he left.

Indeed, Sam thought, looking toward the politician who was now sitting on the sofa in front of the television set, cupping a fresh glass of scotch in both hands.

"Look at those numbers," he said, smiling widely, looking around the room as if he were only now realizing that everyone else had left.

Before his little group gets here, Sam thought, maybe I can get some more information out of him.

"Carlos," she said gently, waiting for a commercial break on the TV. "Kevin said that you'd promised that you and he and Jean would be a family. I guess that was pretty important to him."

He shrugged. "Kids need to hear certain things. It's what I do, Sam. I tell people what they want to hear. I had no idea Kevin would ever take his desire that far."

Voices sounded at the door just then and Sam opened it.

An hour later, with the election a certainty. Tafoya's campaign manager suggested that it was time for him to go down to the ballroom and give his speech. Sam stayed behind in the suite as the rest of them left. She needed a few minutes of silence before being overtaken by the tidal wave of excitement downstairs.

A bright yellow banner across the television screen caught her attention and she un-muted the sound.

"Shocking news from Taos County this evening . . ." The newscaster's voice held a somber tone as the pictures began to flash on screen. Beau leading Kevin Calendar out of the hotel in handcuffs. How had the media gotten hold of this so quickly? She watched until the story had run out of facts and the journalist began to repeat himself. So far, all they had for sure was that a young volunteer in the Tafoya campaign had been arrested.

The picture switched again and the voiceover promised live coverage of the governor-elect's speech, right after the break.

Sam turned it off and left the suite.

In the ballroom the mood was frenetic. A band played rock music with a heavy beat and the mesmerized crowd were waving their arms overhead, swaying and chanting to the tempo. She stood to the side, near one of the massive carved doors.

From the front of the room, a cheer went up, moving through the huge ballroom like a tsunami. Carlos Tafoya stepped from behind a curtain, waving widely and smiling his familiar grin. He took the podium and let the cheers go on for a full three minutes.

When he finally raised his hands, signaling for silence, Sam was likely the only one in the room who noticed the faint whiteness around his mouth, the haunted look in his eyes. If anyone else noticed it was undoubtedly, after all, because the man had just lost his loving wife this past week, the woman with whom he'd planned to share this moment.

"Good evening, New Mexico!" Carlos shouted, and the speech was on.

Sam watched, amazed that he pulled it off. His wife dead, his son going away in handcuffs less than an hour ago, and himself in danger of being pulled into the whole mess. Somehow, she knew the man before this room tonight would come away unscathed, although his unsuspecting son might very well never be free again. A plea bargain—Kevin's life for an admission of manslaughter—it wouldn't be the first time something like had happened in northern New Mexico.

As Carlos went on, reiterating his promises for the state,

Sam closed her eyes, working to regain a bit of the energy that had flowed out of her during the evening. When she opened them again, she saw Sandy Greene, the reporter, watching her.

An image popped into Sam's head—Sandy standing near a door, listening. On the door, some lettering: Suite A. The reporter's rapt attention to the male voice ranting behind the closed barrier of wood. Suddenly Sam knew exactly how the story had become the startling 'news flash' heard round the wires.

A chill crept over her arms and she wanted nothing more than to be out of there. During one of the louder outbursts from the crowd, Sam opened the tall, heavy door beside her and stepped out into the corridor. At the front desk she asked them to call a taxi.

By nine o'clock Sam was drifting off, wrapped in her fleece robe with a mug of hot chocolate on the table beside the sofa. She'd switched on the television to catch the results of a few other races—congressional seats were at stake, along with some legislators. The Albuquerque station continued to rehash the little bit they knew about the arrest of Kevin Calendar but it wasn't much and even the newscasters were tiring of saying the same things and showing a picture of the outside of the Taos jail, quiet and dark this time of night. Across the bottom of the screen, they ran results of the county races and she noticed that Orlando Padilla had, indeed, been re-elected sheriff by a landslide.

She heard the kitchen door close and Kelly called out.

"Beau isn't home yet," she told Sam, "but Iris is snug

in her bed and I wasn't needed so I decided to come home. What was the story on the radio about Taos County and the new governor? I only caught a bit of it."

Sam filled her in on the basics, leaving out everything having to do with witchy predictions, colored auras and the fact that Kevin had tried to attack her before Beau brought him down. There are some things a daughter doesn't need to know.

Kelly said goodnight and Sam headed for her own room, after checking the doors and turning out the lights. She had no idea how much time had passed, only that she was in a complete blackout sleep, when the phone rang.

She felt around for the bedside phone and mumbled a sleepy hello.

"You meddling bitch!"

Chapter 26

Sam came instantly awake.

"Can't believe how you, you slimy bitch . . . how you messed me up." The words were slurred and the voice was definitely Orlando Padilla's.

"Sheriff, what's going on?"

"You know, you—"

"No. Stop just a minute. I don't know. What are you talking about?" Her thoughts tried to wrap themselves around his accusation. He'd been nowhere near the Tafoya victory party tonight.

"Marg . . . Margaret is going to leave me, and it's all your fault."

Ah, the affair with Elena Tafoya was about to come to light. "How is it my fault, Orlando?"

"You just . . . just . . . I don't know what you said to her."

His words became more sloppy and rambling as he went. Her denials that she'd said anything at all to his wife went unheeded. Sam couldn't make any sense of how he thought she was involved and she finally gave him a quick goodbye and hung up the phone.

It rang again almost instantly but she hung up again when she realized that Padilla wouldn't give up. She left the receiver off the hook and tried hard to get back to sleep, but she couldn't get her mind to settle down. Would he come to her house? Would he take out his anger on Beau? Might he even become abusive with Margaret?

Obviously, his brief affair with Elena was about to come to light and here was a guy who didn't want to face the consequences. Sam grumbled a little and rolled over once more, falling asleep—finally—sometime near dawn.

Wednesday morning she gave herself over to the luxury of burrowing into the quilts for an extra hour. With Becky back at the bakery today, both of the younger women had persuaded Sam not to come in early. After the drama of last evening and the interruption to her sleep, it didn't take a lot of will power to let herself sleep in.

Somewhere around nine she began to feel hungry. She pulled on a robe and placed the receiver back on the phone, then went to the kitchen for cereal. The morning television shows were full of talk about the election results, with more and more connections between Carlos Tafoya and Kevin Calendar coming out by the hour. Sam planted herself in a corner of the sofa and crunched on her breakfast as she watched.

The newly elected governor stood before a blue background in some office somewhere, taking questions from the press. In short, it looked like he was taking the tired old "It was inappropriate behavior" line, admitting that he'd once (he made it sound like sometime in a previous life) had an extramarital affair and that there was a child with this other woman. About the time he was getting into the equally tired line about "getting on with the business of the state" Sam's phone rang.

"Hey you," said Beau. "You doing okay this morning?"

He sounded haggard, and admitted that he'd not slept all night when Sam asked how he was.

"Kevin actually admitted quite a bit before Carlos showed up with a lawyer for the kid."

"I've just been watching the spin version on TV," she said. "No doubt he'll not lose his public support, once he's fed them the old boys-will-be-boys routine and expressed just enough remorse."

"Oh, I'm sure of that. When we questioned him, Carlos actually did seem horrified that Kevin took it as far as he did. Apparently, Jean had kept her son in the dark all these years—made up some story about a father who left when he was an infant. She finally broke down last year and told him the truth. Once he found out who his real father was, Kevin *really* wanted them to be a family. Showing Carlos what a good son he'd turned out to be was the whole reason he volunteered with the campaign."

"Seriously? At twenty, this young man thinks they'll just go back in time and become a happy little trio?"

"Well, no one ever said the kid didn't have issues. A lot of them. And it didn't help that Carlos played along, letting Kevin believe that he would leave Elena and marry Jean."

Sam shook her head. What a mess.

"So, one down and one to go," Beau said.

"That's right—Bram Fenton's death. Did Kevin also have something to do with that?"

"Not as far as I can tell. But when I ran the name past Carlos, he sure clammed up."

"What? He didn't hire Fenton after all?"

"I'm still pretty sure he did. Jean Calendar said something weird. She claimed that a man—whom she described very well as Fenton—had been following her for days. She thought Carlos had something do to with it because it started just a couple days after she'd contacted him and told him she was in town."

"Wait a second. Now I'm really confused," Sam said. "Did he hire the investigator to follow Elena or to follow Jean?"

"Well, that's part of what I'm calling you about. You still have Fenton's notebook. Can you go through and re-read, now that we know more about all the players in this case? See if you can find information in Fenton's own notes?"

With a new mission for the day, Sam got out the notebook and set to work on it as soon as they'd ended the phone call. The dates, described with decimal points, were easy to spot now and she quickly located the timeframe for the past few months. As she perused the sets of letters, it all began to fall into place. An hour later she thought she had the answers.

A quick shower, fresh clothes, and she was on her way to Beau's office. She found him with his head on his desk, catching a quick snooze. He raised bloodshot eyes when he heard her approach.

"Sorry. I should have called first," she said.

"I'm glad you're here. I have to stay until the next shift

starts and it's gonna take a lot to keep me awake that long."

"Maybe this will help." She set the notebook down on his desk. "See this? JC is Jean Calendar. Look: '9.15flwdjc' and '9.30pusrvljc@hm.fl2intm'. On September 15, Fenton followed Jean. On the 30th he meant to pick up surveillance at her home and follow to intimidate her. I found instances of these same codes used throughout the book—srvl for surveil, flw meaning to follow someone.

"This proves that Carlos hired Fenton to follow Jean and if possible to frighten her away from Taos and from him. Carlos couldn't afford for her to be revealing his old secrets before the election. I guess he thought that if Jean left town, Kevin would too. Naïve thinking, yes. But people do stupid things under pressure.

"Here . . ." she flipped a page, "are Fenton's notes when he began the surveillance, about Jean's appearance. He describes her in terms that could easily describe Elena, too. Think about it, Beau. Both women have blond hair cut in similar styles, and were very close in height and build . . . I think the night Fenton died, he'd accidentally followed the wrong woman."

"Oh, god, that fits." Beau rummaged through his interview notes. "Last night, Jean told me that Elena once came to her house, sometime in September, to confront her and say that there would be no split with Carlos during the campaign. That he couldn't afford the scandal of a second family at that time, that Jean should just leave town. Elena suggested that Jean stay low-key for a year or so and then there could be a quiet, civilized divorce."

"So . . . Fenton was watching the house. Maybe he didn't see Elena arrive but he did see her leave. Thought it was

Jean, followed, intentionally putting her into a panic. But then Elena had a knife in her purse . . . He wasn't ready for that."

"But Elena told you that she'd been to see her lover that night."

"Maybe she had. She might have come from seeing him, decided to take care of Carlos's little indiscretion herself by reasoning with Jean . . ."

"Like a scandal about her own affair wouldn't cause just as much havoc as Carlos's old affair?"

Sam sighed. "Who knows what she was thinking. She admitted to me that she'd tried to break it off but just couldn't help herself. She *needed* this man."

"What's up?" The male voice intruded sharply. Sam looked up to see that Orlando Padilla had entered the squad room from a side door.

Beau gestured toward his stacks of notes. "Just putting a few loose ends together on the Tafoya case. Trying to piece together what happened with that private investigator case, Bram Fenton."

The sheriff gave him a sharp look. "The suicide off the bridge?"

Beau's eyes narrowed warily. "It wasn't a suicide, remember? The MI found a slashed artery. Guy bled out all over his trench coat."

Sam watched closely. Padilla's outwardly smooth manner couched a vibrating bundle of nerves. The man fairly jangled with tension. The pieces fell neatly into place.

"*You* were Elena's lover." She stated it simply.

Words of denial automatically surfaced. He shuffled a little.

"No," Sam said. "It's true. Everything fits with what Elena told me herself."

His face went white. "She didn't tell you anything."

"She did. She was practically addicted to you, willing to risk everything just to be with you." Even as she uttered the words, Sam had a hard time accepting the fact. This pudgy, lazy man . . . the comparison with the sleek demeanor of Carlos Tafoya didn't even bear mentioning. But things were usually deeper than they seemed, and in matters of the heart who knew what went on.

"And now I know what happened to Bram Fenton, too. Elena must have panicked. She slashed out at a man who'd been following her, just thinking she could make him back off. But when she actually hit him, got the carotid artery and he began to bleed and then to die right there on the street, she needed help, fast. She called the one person she thought she could count on. You. I'll bet the records show that you were on duty that night, so you came to her location, bundled up the body, and carried him to the bridge."

Padilla began looking around for an exit, but Beau quietly disarmed him and stood ready to get physical if need be.

"You couldn't take the risk of dumping the body with the trench coat on it because it would be very evident that blood all around the neck area wasn't consistent with a fall from the bridge. You even added a few more cuts, thinking the medical investigator would probably mistake them for injuries from the rocks below." Sam paused to let the images catch up with her.

"Sam, what about the coat?" Beau asked. "How did it get out to Cheryl Adams's house?"

"I saw him, Beau. Remember the vision I had that day? I told you I'd seen a man in dark clothing putting something into the closet? Check the dates. I'll bet the sheriff was supposed to deliver the eviction notice to Cheryl Adams, and it probably happened within a day or so after Fenton's death. Cheryl's house was left unlocked—I found it that way myself. I'm betting that when Sheriff Padilla got there Cheryl had already moved out, but the house was unlocked. He saw the perfect chance to get rid of the coat in all that clutter. Just hang it in a closet and someone would eventually come along to clean out the place and the coat could never be tied to him."

She turned to the sheriff. "You would have been better off to burn it."

Padilla looked chagrined.

Beau piped up. "You would have been *better* off to turn it in. If you'd reported the death as an accident, you wouldn't be facing charges of tampering with evidence, concealing a murder, aiding and abetting . . . we can probably think of a few more."

Padilla's eyes were searching the room, looking for a way out of his troubles. His gaze landed on the pistol which Beau had taken from him minutes earlier.

"Don't even think about it," Beau warned.

Padilla spun and dashed for the back door, flinging papers off of desks and tipping chairs over as he ran. But Beau was quicker. With one leap he tackled the sheriff and brought him to the floor. From the dispatch area a secretary and another deputy came running.

By the time they reached the tangle of arms and legs, Beau had latched his cuffs onto Padilla's wrists.

Chapter 27

Chocolate buttercream frosting plopped onto the top of the quarter-sheet that Sam had promised for the chocoholics book group this afternoon. She smoothed it with a spatula, creating a flat backdrop for the molded chocolate decorations she and Becky had created yesterday. They'd made a miniature vignette of the bookshop itself, with rows of books—all done in dark, milk and white chocolate—the sales counter with a small chocolate Ivan at the desk, the deep chairs where customers curled up to read sample chapters—Sam's raspberry chocolate almost looked like the plush burgundy upholstery on the real ones.

It had been two weeks since the election, a very interesting two weeks. Details of the bizarre story continued to come out, as national media descended upon their small town to poke and prod and ask questions. Beau withheld a lot of the particulars that would have to come out later, in court but Sam, privy to the dead private investigator's notes, had accumulated more proof against both the new governor and the sheriff. Although Padilla had won re-election to his office, for the moment he was on suspension and being investigated by the internal affairs division of the department.

Sandy Greene, the reporter who'd been first to break the story at the state level, was immediately fired from her job. A fine thanks, Sam thought, but no doubt sparked by the fact that the newspaper's owner was a close friend and large contributor to Carlos Tafoya. He gained nothing by trying to quash the spunky young reporter. The firing made the news headlines even larger, and Sandy was quickly snapped up by a television network affiliate in Denver. She'd called Sam to tell her about the advancement in her career and the increase in pay. Some things do end up being all right.

Meanwhile, as Sam set tiny chocolate figurines of Ivan's bookstore customers—including herself and Riki and Zoë—in place, she reflected on the way in which Carlos Tafoya was coming out of the whole thing amazingly unscathed. But then, wasn't that the way with politicians?

She heard voices out in the sales area and looked up from her work to see Victor Tafoya pushing his way through to the kitchen. Her wizened, old landlord had already expressed his displeasure over her role in disgracing his son, as if Sam had actually committed some crime, herself. He shuffled over to her work table, not bothering to remove the battered straw hat that glistened with melting snowflakes.

"Here," he grumbled, shoving a folded sheet of paper at her.

"What's this, Victor?" She set down her pastry bag and

wiped her hands on a damp towel before reaching out to take the page.

"You're evicted."

"What!" Her heart crashed. "You can't do that! I have a lease."

"Not anymore." He jammed his hands against his skinny hips. "I don't need troublemakers like you around."

"Mr. Taf—"

"Be out by Friday!"

Sam stood frozen to the spot as he stomped out.

"Whoa." Becky looked just as immovable as Sam.

Sam shook herself and dashed after him. "Wait, you've got no real cause to throw me out."

"So, sue me!" He yanked the front door open, sending the bells into a clamor.

Jen stood behind the counter, wide-eyed. "Can he do that?"

Sam's veins felt like ice. She'd worked so hard to get the shop open and build her clientele. She could find another location but she loved being here, next to the bookstore and so close to the plaza. Tears threatened to spill.

Outside, fine sleet pelted the elder Tafoya as he jerked open the door to his ratty old pickup truck. Why the father of the new governor didn't at least drive a decent vehicle was always the subject of speculation, but at this point Sam couldn't even give it a thought. The engine cranked and cranked in the blustery November day, but it wouldn't start. She could see him cursing it. He pounded a fist against the steering wheel. Then his face went very pale and he clutched at his chest.

"Uh-oh." Sam watched as he slumped over the wheel,

setting off the horn. "Call an ambulance."

She dashed out the door, hit by a blast of cold air, but she didn't pause. She reached the door of the truck about the same time as three other people who'd heard the blast of the old horn.

"Sam, what's up?" Riki asked, wiping her hands on a towel. She still had shampoo suds on her plastic apron.

"He must be having a heart attack. Jen's calling for help."

"I also have dialed the 911," said Ivan Petrenko, emerging from the bookstore.

Sirens sounded nearby, coming from the fire station that was only two blocks away. Within a minute, paramedics were at work on Victor Tafoya and the neighbors huddled under the purple awning at Sweet's Sweets. The awning that would have to be fitted to a new window. Sam felt her eyes begin to prickle again.

"Miss Samantha, is all right. See? Is breathing with the mask thing."

"Oh, Ivan, I know. It's not that."

Riki, too, hovered near Sam and with her friends nearby, the emotion let go. She waved them inside her shop where Jen was already pouring lattes all around.

"Mr. Tafoya just gave us an eviction notice," Jen told Riki and Ivan, as they all took seats at one of the tables.

"Eviction! Well, that is just not going to happen," Riki said, the Americanism sounding cute with her accent. "Is it, now, Ivan?"

"*Certainement pas.* Fight this we shall do!"

"How?" Sam moaned. "I can't afford to take him to court and drag this out. Plus, now that his son will be in the governor's office, there's no way I'd win."

"Let me work on it," Riki said. "The old man is a branch of the same tree as his son. He's been hitting on me ever since I moved into this building. Well, as they say, two can play at that game."

Sam laughed at the image of petite, twenty-something Riki flirting with the seventy-five year old Tafoya and the tension was broken.

"I've got to finish Ivan's cake," she said, picking up her mug. "You stay and finish your coffee."

Riki stood, as well. "I shall be visiting our landlord in hospital, right after I finish bathing Toodles—oh no, I left Rasper under the dryer!" She abandoned her latte and dashed out.

By four o'clock Sam had put Tafoya's threat into perspective. Between momentary bouts of tears, she decided that if she were forced to move she could do it.

Meanwhile, she'd been too busy to dwell on it. Most of the ambulance watchers had migrated into the shop for pastries and coffee, so the morning had passed quickly. Working on auto-pilot, Sam finished three more custom orders and mixed up dough for afternoon cookies which always came out of the oven as the school kids began walking by on their way home. The chocoholics cake had turned out beautifully and she carried it to the front when Ivan walked into her shop.

Riki came in just as Ivan had finished giving lengthy praise of the way Sam and Becky had duplicated the layout of his store in chocolate. "Is too beautiful to eat," he kept saying.

"I must say, I think he's right," Riki said.

"Well, you decide what you want to do. It won't keep forever," Sam told them.

"Oh, Sam, by the way, I think I have news that will make you happy."

"You talked to Mr. Tafoya?" Sam held her breath.

"In a way."

"Ohmygod, you didn't . . ."

Riki's face screwed up in a grimace. "Get physical? As you Yanks would say, yuk!! I can't imagine it."

Sam chuckled out loud.

"No. Basically, I threatened him. Sort of told him that if he evicts you, he might as well put up three 'To Let' signs because Ivan and I would move out as well."

Ivan looked a bit panicky at that news.

"And he caved?" Sam asked.

"Indeed. In this economy he can't exactly afford to lose three tenants in one day. And it's not like he would put any of us out of business—there are plenty of empty retail spaces in this town at the moment." She gave a smug smile. "I might have also mentioned that we have a connection or two in the media these days."

"So I'm staying?" Sam still couldn't quite believe it.

"We're all staying." Riki gave her a long hug and Ivan murmured something in Russian that involved making the sign of the cross. He took his cake and scooted out the door.

Sam hugged Riki again as the younger woman headed back to her dogs. She held the door for a customer who had her arms full with a boxed sheet cake.

"Have a magical day!" Jen called out to the woman.

Sam raised an eyebrow as the door closed. "Magical?"

"Absolutely. People always mention the special feeling they get in here, the 'magic.' I just pass it along."

Jen polished the rounded glass on the antique display

case. "Think about it, Sam. Magic is everywhere. I feel so lucky to stand here and watch the sun rise over the mountain every morning. There's magic in those big fat snowflakes out there or in golden leaves against a brilliant blue sky."

"And in that freshest of greens when the trees leaf out in spring?"

"You got it. People just have to look for the magic—I'm only reminding them."

Sam looked around her shop, taking in the display cases, the smell of fresh rich coffee and spicy chai, the café tables and chairs where customers often lingered with their morning papers and indulged in a second pastry. The windows showcased her latest creations and the beveled glass door and purple awning in front gave the shop the ambiance she'd envisioned for years before it actually opened. Her vision had manifested itself with every bit of the special feeling for which she'd hoped.

Beau walked in, to find her dabbing at her eyes. "What's this?"

After Sam gave the condensed version of the day's drama, he smiled. "Well, I have a little good news, myself." He straightened and pointed at the badge on his chest.

"Sheriff?" Sam said. "They've made you sheriff?"

"Acting, temporary sheriff. Somebody has to run things until Padilla's done facing the music."

"So, can I hug the sheriff?" She put her arms around his neck before he answered.

Outside, the snowflakes had grown fatter, falling like downy feathers, giving the shrubs a powdered sugar feel. Jen was right. Magic.

More stories with Samantha and Friends!

Samantha Sweet breaks into houses for a living.
But she's really a baker with a magical touch, who
invites you to her delightful pastry shop—
Sweet's Sweets.
Don't miss the next book in this series!

Holiday Sweets

It's the Christmas season and a chocolatier shows up
at Sam's shop, offering to create a special line of hand-
dipped chocolates for her customers. He is willing to
work for no pay, just to prove himself.
But when she learns that he has connections to the
wooden box that seems to give Sam her mystical
powers, she learns that dark forces may do just about
anything to take it away from her.

Connie Shelton is the author of the bestselling Charlie Parker mysteries and now the Samantha Sweet mystery series. She has taught writing—both fiction and nonfiction—and is the creator of the Novel In A Weekend™ writing course. She lives in northern New Mexico.

Made in the USA
Lexington, KY
29 June 2011